HEATHER BOYD

USA TODAY BESTSELLING AUTHOR

SAINTS AND SINNERS

THE LADY TAMED

SAINTS AND SINNERS

Book 1: The Duke and I
Book 2: A Gentleman's Vow
Book 3: An Earl of Her Own
Book 4: The Lady Tamed

The characters and events portrayed in this book are fictitious. Any similarity to real persons, living or dead, is purely coincidental and not intended by the author.

Dedication

To Kelli Collins, my glorious editor who works tirelessly to make me a better writer. Thank you for the corrections, moral support and just being you.

Chapter One

F anny Rivers fixed a diamond necklace about her throat and then dropped her hands to consider the effect in the mirror. The style was perfect for the gown she wore but perhaps not so for the coming gathering. "A little too much for a luncheon, I think."

"Any would be my choice," declared Mrs. Jessica Whitfield, Fanny's younger sister.

"No." Fanny removed the necklace and chose instead a long gold chain with a teardrop pearl hanging from it. She fastened the chain about her neck and settled the pearl between her breasts. She smiled. Perfection.

"*Come on, Fanny.* There's got to be steam coming out of her ears by now," Jessica warned with growing impatience from the doorway of Fanny's old chambers at Stapleton Manor, her father's home.

Fanny was visiting her father's country estate for the second time this year, to attend the wedding of her younger sister. Her first visit had been for Jessica's wedding to neighbor Gideon Whitfield in June. The second wedding would be for Rebecca's marriage to Lord Rafferty a week from now—and *that* announcement had come as quite a shock.

"We're not late, and besides, it doesn't hurt to make the man Rebecca is marrying a little anxious for her whereabouts," Fanny promised.

Jessica uttered a wicked chuckle. "He's anxious for the wedding night."

"And all the ones after, too," Fanny promised and then laughed along with her sister. Rebecca and Adam, Earl of Rafferty, made an unlikely pair. But having come across them together in an unguarded moment Fanny should never have witnessed, she understood. Her sister had finally been swept up in a grand passion. "Have you ever seen a more smitten man?"

Jessica grinned. "Yes, my husband looks at me like that every morning."

Gideon Whitfield, Jessica's husband, at least tried to keep his passionate regard for his wife off his face at mealtimes. "And are we not all happy about his constancy. Rivers was much the same, too."

"I hardly remember your late husband now," Jessica admitted.

Fanny missed Rivers still, especially at family gatherings. "Well, he adored you. Thought you would grow up and break hearts."

Jessica blushed a little.

Fanny, deciding she was as ready as she'd ever be, collected her shawl and reticule and swept toward the door. She did not dislike the institution of marriage. She had enjoyed a happy, if brief, one herself. But the urge to take the plunge a second time was not appealing. She had been left with a vast fortune when her husband had died. Fortune hunters had come out of the woodwork the day she'd cast her mourning aside. And that was five long years ago now. She had learned to do without a husband, if not a man in her bed from time to time.

She tweaked Jessica's nose. "Are you ready?"

"An hour ago."

"Come on, we're very late," Fanny murmured.

"You made us late," Jessica grumbled as she darted out to wait for Fanny to secure her bedchamber door and pocket the key. There were many guests staying at Stapleton Manor for the wedding, and Fanny liked knowing her papers and possessions were always secure.

She strolled along the hall at an unhurried pace, despite Jessica's attempt to hurry her along. At the top of the stairs, she paused to look down. Rebecca was standing at the foot of the stairs sixteen feet below, arms crossed under her breasts. "Good morning, sister," Fanny called as she started down the grand mahogany staircase to meet her.

Rebecca punched her hands to her hips and glared. "I was about to leave without you."

"You would not dare," Fanny murmured soothingly. Rebecca and Jessica were matched in impatience today. "Not without your favorite sisters by your side."

"My only sisters," Rebecca shot back just as quickly. "Come on, Ava will think we've forgotten about the party."

Ava was Lord Rafferty's only daughter and quite excited to have a new mother soon.

"As if we could," Jessica exclaimed. "I am very much looking forward to spending time at your future home. I've visited Gable Park so rarely."

Rebecca hooked her arm through Jessica's and strolled out the front door, nodding to the Stapleton butler as she passed. "Well, that will not be the case after I wed, I hope."

"No," Jessica promised.

"Of course, we will visit." Now when Fanny came to the country, she'd have to extend her stays by almost two weeks in order to visit three homes instead of just her father's.

Rebecca climbed into the carriage first with an audible huff and immediately started fiddling with the fit of her gown's bodice, and not for the first time this week, either. Her clothes had apparently and suddenly become snug. Fanny observed her sister discreetly, seeking more confirmation that Rebecca might be in the family way before she embarrassed her by asking. Always highly strung, Rebecca had cast up her accounts that very morning though blamed it on nerves. If there was a babe coming, her marriage to Rafferty couldn't come a moment too soon.

Jessica settled into the seat beside Fanny. "When can we expect to meet your beau?"

"He is not really my beau," she reminded her youngest sister.

Rebecca huffed. "Fanny didn't want Lord Letterford to think he stood a chance, so what does she do but hire a paid companion to come between them."

"He's an actor," Fanny corrected. "And a very good actor."

Rebecca's nose wrinkled with distaste as she mouthed "*actor*" as if the profession was offensive. "An unknown. Could you not have found someone more believable? Someone feted and familiar with our circle would have been my preference."

Fanny thought she'd been rather clever. She'd hired a talented man to pretend to be her most ardent admirer, and therefore, always by her side—between her and any fortune hunter's intent on wooing her. Of course, no one would believe for a moment that she'd ever seriously consider a marriage to someone who trod the boards for a living, but they might believe she'd engage in a bit of scandal with one...therefore scaring off her most ardent suitors.

"I think it is a brilliant idea," Jessica enthused. "Lord Letterford is always asking Giddy if he's seen or heard that you would be visiting us soon. I don't want him for a brother."

Fanny shook her head. "My opinion of him hasn't changed since I was a girl. If he proposes again, I will refuse again."

"I think he must be very lonely," Jessica suggested.

Fanny caught Rebecca's eye. "Is there anything left for me to do for you before the wedding takes place?"

"I shouldn't think so. We just need the last guests to arrive," Rebecca replied with a heavy sigh. "Most have come, but there are a few stragglers. Your beau, for example, since you insist he be placed beside you at nearly every meal."

Fanny inclined her head. "Mr. Dawes arrives today."

Complete with a new wardrobe Fanny had paid for to make his presence among the wedding guests less of a talking point. The young man she'd singled out for her patronage would make a perfect companion for all the dinners and balls and such amusements that had been arranged to celebrate the marriage of Rebecca and Lord Rafferty. Father had been adamant that no expense be spared— most likely because he'd been allowed to do so little for Rebecca's first celebration.

The trip from Stapleton to Lord Rafferty's home, Gable Park, lasted a good long while, and Fanny talked with her sisters about everything and nothing, the way they had as girls.

By the time they reached the mansion, Fanny was feeling the need to speak with other people. Her sisters took too much of an interest in her unmarried state, and she was feeling the pressure to conform.

Thankfully, Lord Rafferty and his daughter were waiting for their arrival. The pair swept open the carriage door and hustled the blushing bride-to-be out. They exchanged greetings and then Rafferty drew Rebecca aside. When she heard kissing behind her, Fanny didn't bother to turn and chide the pair for their behavior. They were always locked at the lips of late, as they should be in her opinion.

Fanny caught Jessica's eye. "We had better find our own way inside without them."

Jessica nodded.

They entered a large hall arm in arm and were directed toward the drawing room, where guests were milling about talking in small groups. The Duchess of Stapleton, Gillian, was on the far side of the room talking with a couple Fanny didn't immediately recognize.

She turned to Jessica. "How about we take a turn about the room?"

But Jessica had caught sight of her husband standing across the room, and her face lit up with love. "Would you excuse me?"

"Do I have a choice?"

"No." Jessica kissed her cheek, then abandoned Fanny with a laugh, meeting Gideon Whitfield halfway across the room. They didn't kiss, but it was clear they were thinking about it, given how they smiled at each other's lips.

Fanny felt a tiny pang of envy.

"Ah, young love. Isn't it wonderful?"

Fanny winced inwardly and then turned to face the man she'd most hoped to avoid today. "Lord Letterford."

He rubbed his hands together. "Now it really is a celebration. But her grace was just telling me that your father will not be joining us today. Surely that cannot be true."

"Yes, I'm afraid it is," she promised, eying the crowd in the hope of rescue.

Letterford drew closer. "Nothing seriously wrong, I trust."

"No." Fanny waved her hand about, discreetly shifting her body farther away from his. "A matter on the estate required his attention, I believe."

Letterford sighed. "I'm glad to hear it, for it wouldn't do to have two estates in distress."

Fanny frowned at him. "What other estate is in distress?"

"All is not well with Hawthorne, I hear," Letterford whispered.

Fanny hadn't heard a word of it from anyone at home. "I'm sure that is not true."

"I hope you are right," Letterford said. "But my servants say otherwise. Bad health might yet take one of our dearest neighbors."

Servants often knew there was trouble before anyone else. She would have to squeeze in a visit to the Hawthornes' tomorrow, confirm all was well, and put an end to any rumors.

Jessica and Gideon strolled past, arm in arm,

and Fanny frowned when they disappeared outside together.

"Now, don't begrudge the pair their happiness," Letterford murmured. "You and I know love is all too fleeting. Let her have this happy time, for we both know it ends all too soon."

Unfortunately, that was true.

Letterford offered his arm, and Fanny, seeing no chance of diversion, resigned herself to being stuck with him for a while. Rebecca, Rafferty, and Ava hurried past, laughing together, and Fanny wished she might follow, but Letterford was as slow as an ancient drake. "I never thought there was a man brave enough to take on Mrs. Warner and smile about it."

"He knows her nature very well."

"Yes, practically grown up together," Letterford said.

"Hardly that," Fanny chided. "But he has been a regular visitor to Stapleton and my father for some years, like yourself. I'm sure he's well prepared to make a second match."

Rafferty would be her father's second friend to end up married to one of his daughters, too. Fanny vowed not to be the third to fall foul of that dangerous trend.

Fanny wished she'd arranged for Mr. Dawes to travel with her instead of waiting for his new wardrobe to be delivered to him. She'd not known the extent of the wedding festivities until after her arrival. "Lady Rivers, I wonder if I might consult you on a matter of grave importance to me."

Please do not propose to me for a second time, I beg of you!

Fanny winced but then out of the corner of her eye, she spotted Gillian, Duchess of Stapleton, watching her and Letterford talking. Gillian beckoned Fanny to join her, and it appeared to Fanny imperative that she go. "Forgive me but it seems I am being summoned by the duchess. Would you excuse me?"

Lord Letterford's shoulders sagged. "Of course, perhaps we might talk again later."

Not if I can help it. Fanny smiled politely. "I look forward to it."

But she fully intended to go out of her way to avoid the earl for the rest of the day so he could not finish asking a question that he'd only receive a negative answer to. She would not marry Letterford to cheer him up, restore his fortunes, or fund any improvements to his estate or back an unwise investment.

Fanny caught up her friend and new mama's outstretched hands and held them. "What is wrong," she murmured.

"The babe is kicking again, and I'm in danger of laughing out loud." Gillian squeezed her fingers. "Lord Thwaite's eyes kept dipping to my stomach as the babe moved. He seemed horrified and kept asking if I needed a chair. Do children not know there's a time and place for this sort of thing?"

"Apparently not." Fanny looked down at Gillian's stomach. "Quiet, infant. Your mother is supposed to be composed and regal today."

Gillian sighed after a minute. "At last. Peace and stillness. You wield the voice of authority so well. Your father's presence has the same affect."

"I *am* the eldest."

"When your brother Samuel arrived and spoke to me, I had to quickly seat myself. Obviously, the child is looking forward to meeting his stepbrother a little too much."

Fanny laughed. "Poor darling. Not long now."

"Oh, I do hope so."

Jessica suddenly stopped in front of them. "You need to go to Rebecca, Fanny. She's in the dining room on the verge of…well, you know how she can be."

"I'll take care of it," Fanny promised.

She left Gillian and found Rebecca and a harassed-looking pair of maids stammering out repeated apologies. Fanny closed the doors behind her and raised her voice a little. "Mrs. Warner?"

Rebecca spun about, eyes wild. "Do you see this?"

"What has overset you?"

"The flowers. Can you not see? They just get taller and taller. It's ruined the whole effect."

Fanny glanced about the room. Rebecca was something of a perfectionist and obviously determined that the wedding be nothing short of spectacular. The flowers were cut much too tall for a seated dinner party. Not quite a disaster, but clearly Rebecca saw it that way.

Fanny sighed, took up her sister's hands and held them tightly. "I'll take care of it."

Rebecca sagged. "Would you?"

"Happy to help. I can handle a pair of shears." She steered her sister toward the door. "Now go back to the guests and that ridiculous man you love, and for heaven's sake, stop worrying. Enjoy yourself."

There'd be a pre-wedding dinner and a pre-wedding party as well, but each occasion would be unique. Today was merely a rehearsal for married life.

"What would I do without you."

"Pray you never have to find out," Fanny joked, pushing Rebecca out the door and closing it in her face.

Fanny turned to the maids and shrugged. "You'd never guess she's been married before. Please forgive her. She wants so much to make everything perfect for Lord Rafferty."

The pair nodded. "We understand, my lady. To be honest, we were afraid she'd burst into tears."

"Well, let's not have that. Now, we will each need a pair of shears. Quickly now."

One raced off, and the other followed Fanny to a nearby vase as she studied the arrangements. "There really are just too many vases."

One maid winced. "Lord Rafferty kept saying

he wanted lots of Mrs. Warner's favorite flowers, my lady."

"Oh, dear. I'm sure he meant well but…well, let's keep a few of the taller ones intact for his sake, but place them over there on the mantle above the hearth and another few about the permitter of the room on the other furniture. Then we must shorten the table arrangements."

Working together, they found a better height and carefully trimmed all the table arrangements so that everyone would be able to see each other. It took about half an hour, and by the time they were finished, Fanny vowed never to cut another flower stem again.

She thanked the maids on her sister's behalf and discreetly rejoined the party. Rebecca was standing across the room, hanging on to her betrothed's arm. Fanny caught her eye and gave her a quick and hopefully reassuring smile that all was well.

Lord Letterford was suddenly at Fanny's side. "Do you have a moment now, Lady Rivers?"

A footman announced the luncheon.

Fanny stood aside with him as Rebecca adroitly maneuvered her future husband land guests toward the dining room. "Not really at this moment."

Letterford remained by her elbow as other guests sauntered past. "I understand from the duke that your visit to the country will be a short one again."

"Yes, I am due back in London the week after

next," she confirmed. "I hope to spend a lot of time with my family."

"A pity, for I had hoped for a chance to see more of you."

She smiled. "I'm afraid that will not be possible. Do excuse me again, but I must find my seat for the luncheon."

Lord Letterford beamed, throwing out his chest. "I have the happy honor of sitting by your side today."

Fanny was taken aback. Rebecca had promised she'd not be placed beside Lord Letterford for any event.

Letterford smiled. "Rafferty obliged me and switched my place as a favor."

"Is that so," Fanny said, dying a little inside at the thought of being trapped with a man she had so little in common with.

But there was nothing she could do but make the best of it and hope he didn't propose in front of so many witnesses.

She couldn't wait for tomorrow, when she would have Mr. Dawes by her side again. *He* would not be bribed or tricked into leaving her side for any reason. There were compensations to being a widow with vast resources at her disposal. Loyalty *could* be bought.

"How lucky for me," she managed to force out as they took their seats.

Chapter Two

Jeremy Dawes had never been so far from London in his life. Or willingly remained so close to other human beings for so long, either. Jeremy escaped the close confines of the mail coach for the wide-open space of the Stapleton village square and looked around, uncertain of what he expected but filled with enthusiasm.

The little village was awash with new sights and sound that he drank in. There was a friendliness to the inhabitants that he found reassuring almost immediately. Jeremy quickly concluded that the fine people of this village were unlikely to steal his new hat from his head, or his expensive luggage, but he kept a wary eye out just in case. Thieves were everywhere…and he should know.

Jeremy glanced at the coachmen shouting out a spate of orders to everyone and returned to the conveyance. He was anxious to collect his trunk, aware the quality of workmanship was better than those of most who traveled the public conveyance with him, and that it had marked him as someone worth stealing from. In Jeremy's experience, this had to be the first time ever he'd appeared more prosperous than his fellow man. It was quite a disconcerting situation to find himself in, actually.

Jeremy had been born poor and had expected to be so all his life. He'd scrimped and stolen to get by since he'd been orphaned as a boy, too young to remember he'd had a family once upon a time. He'd found employment at a theater in recent years and enjoyed modest success supporting the lead actors and understudies as he learned the craft of pretending to be someone else. But to get ahead in life, he'd learned that actors needed a patron.

He'd found his…Lady Fanny Rivers. Suddenly having coins to spare in his pocket was very much a novelty still. He had kept his first shilling, to remind himself of where he began. Now he was about to embark on his first role as a leading man in a very private play. His only regret was that no one in the company would ever see his performance.

As baggage was tossed down carelessly, Jeremy rushed to collect his new traveling trunk before it was damaged in the drop. He juggled it as well as the smaller case he'd been given to bring by Lady Rivers' London man of business.

"When you're ready, sir," a man called out.

Jeremy jerked around for the location of that voice and spotted a sour old man watching the coach being unloaded from a nearby gig. Lady Rivers had promised he'd be met and conveyed to her father's estate, rather than having to walk the whole way on foot. The fellow might look unhappy, but he was clearly an upper servant of some sort.

He drew closer to the fellow. No rings on his fingers. A pocket watch on a tarnished chain across his belly. Right-handed. "Are you from Stapleton Manor? Did Lady Rivers send you?"

The fellow paused to suck on his teeth before answering, assessing Jeremy in turn. "I am, and she did."

Relieved he'd not have to wait all day to finish his journey, Jeremy strode forward, smiling. Time to *act*. "Mr. Jeremy Dawes."

The old man raised a brow and then looked him up and down again. "Are you sure? You don't look like one of her usual friends."

"Yes. I am." He frowned though, worried he hadn't perfected his costume. "What do her usual friends usually look like?"

"Useless perfumed tulips, too lazy to wipe their own behinds," the fellow declared.

Well that wasn't him. Jeremy could have set down his own luggage for the man to take care of but the man was older than him, and he wasn't at all lazy to tote his own possessions. He would set himself apart from Lady Rivers' *perfumed* friends by his actions. He set the smaller case on the seat beside the driver and then secured his traveling trunk to the back himself. Once he was sure everything was safe from loss, he clambered up beside the driver and clutched the small case on his lap aware the servant was watching him closely. "When you're ready, sir."

"Sir? Well, now." The man sniffed the air and grunted when he must have detected no trace of perfume in the air. "The name's Fenton. I'm his grace's steward."

Jeremy extended his hand. "A pleasure to meet you."

Fenton looked at it but shook his head. "You're late."

"Not through my actions, I assure you," Jeremy promised. "There's probably been dozens of small delays along the way. People forgetting their luggage. Jumping on and off. Changes of horse. None of which I was involved with personally."

Fenton slapped the reins over the horse's rump, and the carriage lurched forward. Jeremy hadn't been prepared for it and was tossed about. He scrambled to hold fast to Lady Rivers' case, his hat, and the seat, too. "Oi. Have a care!"

Fenton regarded him though narrowed eyes. "Too rough for you?" The fellow looked at him sourly, sucking on his teeth. "She sure can pick 'em."

"I beg your pardon?"

"Never mind." The fellow slapped the reins again, and they moved off at a faster clip. Jeremy kept a hand on his hat to save it from separation with his head. It was the finest hat he'd ever owned and a gift from Lady Rivers, along with everything else he owned.

They'd been driving for twenty minutes before the old man spoke again. "Lady Rivers is away visiting and won't be there to welcome you to Stapleton."

"Oh," Jeremy said, feeling somewhat disappointed. He had hoped to speak to her before he had to mingle with any wedding guests. "When will she be back?"

"No doubt when she's good and ready and not a moment sooner." The fellow kept his eyes on the road ahead. "You'd best remember a woman like her does as she pleases."

Jeremy agreed. He'd already noticed Lady Rivers was an independent, headstrong sort of woman. "Have you worked for the family long?"

The fellow speared him with a suspicious glance. "All my life. I'll be here long after you've gone on your merry way, too, I expect."

Jeremy nodded. His role with Lady Rivers likely wouldn't be of any great duration. One brief moment in the spotlight over the next two weeks and then a quick exit and a return to the theater.

He relaxed a bit more on the seat, but the man at his side kept drawing his attention. He watched his mannerisms, pondering if the man was naturally abrasive or if his prickly tone was strictly reserved for Jeremy. A steward might not normally collect a guest from the mail coach. "Are there many guests staying at Stapleton for the wedding?"

"A few, but the family is settled in and that's all who matter."

Lady Rivers had explained that she had a large family. He had memorized all the names, and connections, so he did not embarrass himself or Lady Rivers.

Fenton sighed. "There she is."

"Where?" Jeremy asked, looking for a carriage or horse carrying his lady in the nearby fields. He was excited to see her again. An actor always needed to please their patron.

"The manor house, paper skull!"

"Oh." Jeremy looked to where the man now pointed. He probably should care that the steward had just insulted him, but he was too surprised by what he was looking at. "Oh, my."

Stapleton was much larger than Lady Rivers had suggested when she'd convinced him to spend a fortnight in the countryside pretending to be her most ardent admirer.

Fenton smiled. "Ain't she the most remarkable sight in all of England?"

Jeremy hardly knew what to say in response. He'd never seen a single structure that could rival it. But there was a lot in the world that Jeremy had never seen or imagined yet. There was a look about the place that spoke of power and wealth. "Lady Rivers never mentioned the size of the house was so vast."

"Course not. Grew up in it, married a man

with another just like it. Ain't you never been to her estate?"

"Not yet."

Fenton squinted at him. "How long you known Lady Rivers?"

"We met at the start of the season."

The fellow slowed the carriage, bringing them to a halt, and just sat there admiring the manor. Finally, he turned to Jeremy. "How long since she started paying for your upkeep then?"

It was commonplace for actors to have wealthy patrons who supported them financially, but Jeremy's cheeks grew hot anyway under Fenton's scrutiny. "She began only last month."

His brows shot up. "Not the same day you met like all the others? I'm surprised she waited so long. The lady is always taking in strays."

Jeremy colored even more. Yes, he was a kept man. Clothed by a rich woman. It was every actor's dream come true. He'd signed a contract. He was hers, and she'd pledged to go along with any scene he felt might be required to ensure her ruse was a complete success. But Jeremy was sure it would not turn out to be as simple as she imagined. No performance was ever free from drama or unexpected mishaps. "She is a very generous patron to those of us in the arts."

"Yes, she most certainly is. The needy and useless flock to her like geese to fallen crumbs."

Clearly Fenton didn't approve of actors. "Can we go?"

Fenton slapped the reins over the horse's rump again and Jeremy's excitement grew.

Yes, Jeremy was as needy and nearly as useless as anyone else in the theater. But at least he wasn't stealing from anyone anymore. He didn't need to. Lady Rivers believed he had promise as an actor, or else she wouldn't have handed him the plum role in her little play. She trusted him.

But one particular thing she had insisted on was that he show respect to everyone employed at her father's estate. Even the grumpy ones, he supposed. He had to win over this Fenton fellow, and make sure he said nothing to detract from his performance later. He smiled, determined to ignore Fenton's sour mood. "Lady Rivers is fond of geese. She keeps one with a broken wing in London. Vicious, evil-tempered thing it is too," Jeremy confided.

Fenton grunted. "Probably too tough to make a decent meal."

He chuckled. "I'd say so. She calls it Fent—"

Jeremy buttoned his lips and shut his eyes briefly in horror. She called the evil thing *Fenton*. Lady Rivers had named the goose after the Stapleton steward, and Jeremy had just told him. How would he react? Insulted?

But Fenton started to laugh and said no more about the naming of the goose as he drove them toward the manor.

Stapleton grew closer and larger. Jeremy started counting windows and had to give up at six and twenty, but there were plenty more to be seen after that number had been surpassed.

They came to a halt before an impossibly wide set of doors.

"Well," Fenton grumbled. "Out you get."

Jeremy climbed down, clutching the small traveling case under his arm. His driver stayed on the bench, and no servants came out to help, so Jeremy had no choice but to retrieve his own trunk from the back of the conveyance. Once he had that, Fenton slapped the reins over his mount's hindquarters again and drove off without another word.

Jeremy stood on the drive, watching him go with annoyance. He was accustomed to being treated rudely in London. He knew what people would believe about him when they met him here, too. He was an outsider, someone who didn't belong. He still found it odd that Lady Rivers had asked him to come to the country and not someone more experienced.

He glanced around slowly, taking in his surroundings. The Stapleton Manor grounds were extensive and very, very empty of people. Eerily empty, in fact. He very much longed to be indoors. "Guess I'll have to knock on the door myself," he muttered under his breath as he started forward.

Before he could pull the bell, the great doors opened wide and a trio of servants trotted out.

A pair of liveried footmen hefted his trunk between them and hurried back inside at a run.

A third man lingered near Jeremy. "May I take that for you, sir?"

The case had been entrusted to him. He'd made a promise to never let it out of his sight for a moment. "No."

"Very good, sir. If you will follow me."

Jeremy entered Stapleton's front hall, prepared for anything, but he couldn't have stopped the whistle that left his lips. He had never seen such a beautiful chamber in all his life, and this was only an entrance hall.

The footman turned to him. "Wait here, please."

"Of course," Jeremy agreed.

He looked around, up at the high walls decorated with plaster moldings of birds and what he assumed were family portraits. A wide staircase rose to the next level, where he'd been told all guests would sleep. Jeremy's last bed had been on the floor in a corner of the stage.

"You must be Mr. Dawes."

Jeremy smiled pleasantly and turned around to find a tall man emerging from a nearby room. He was big, bigger than Jeremy by half a head at least, older by at least a dozen years or so, and might just be the butler. "Indeed I am."

"May I be of assistance?" the fellow asked in a bored voice.

"Yes, well, if you could tell me where I am to go?"

"The servants have taken your trunk up already. I can show you the way."

Relief filled him. "I would appreciate that very much. Thank you."

The man inclined his head and started up the stairs. "This way."

Jeremy followed, encountering no other souls on the way to a large light-filled room with a massive bed placed in the center. He stared at it in shock. At least four of his fellow actors could have shared that bed and been very comfortable still. He could hardly believe the bed, the chamber, would be his for two whole weeks. But his trunk was being unpacked, and his new possessions were already being put away.

The fellow turned to him, one brow lifting. "Was there really just the one trunk?"

"Yes, of course. How many did you expect?"

"Several, I imagined." The fellow prowled about the room, observing the servants at their work and nodding. He turned to Jeremy suddenly. "I'm surprised you've acquired so little, given the length of your association with Lady Rivers. She is usually much more giving to someone like you."

Jeremy straightened to his full height, offended by the remark. "I have everything I need."

The man stroked his long fingers over the trunk's lettering. J. K. D. "What does the K stand for?"

"It is none of your business what my full name is."

"What if I think it is?"

Jeremy was taken aback by the man's tone. "Look, you had better mind your own business and get on with it. Lady Rivers would not be pleased to learn I'd faced an inquisition from you."

The fellow smiled slowly. "Will you tattle on me?"

Jeremy looked the man up and down. "No, but…"

"Lady Rivers is easily taken advantage of," the fellow announced.

"You could say that of everyone."

"And yet you have your hand out to her." The fellow drew close. "Just another attention-seeking fop intent on spending a fortune on fine hats from Lock's and frequenting the very best tailor her money can buy. Weston, I believe you're wearing."

Jeremy brought his face within inches of the fellow's, his hands curling into fists. "Hold your tongue unless you want trouble from me."

"Oh, do you see yourself as a buck then? Do you attend Gentleman Jackson's, too?"

The fellow didn't even look alarmed that he was still being glared at, but the other servants had all paused to watch the confrontation. *They* seemed alarmed.

Jeremy quickly got his temper under control. "No. I'm only an actor, and Lady Rivers my patroness. She is a great lady and spoken of with respect. Especially by those who've known her longer than I probably ever will."

"Got you under her thumb already, has she?" The fellow suddenly grinned. "She's a persistent minx, my daughter. I've yet to meet a man who can say no to her when she gets an idea in her head."

Jeremy blinked several times. "What did you say? Daughter?"

The other servants snickered but *the duke* shushed them. "Enough of that now. Back to work, all of you."

"Oh, my God. I thought you were…" Jeremy bowed deeply, his face flaming as the realization dawned that he was actually standing before the Duke of Stapleton, Lady Rivers' esteemed father. "Forgive me for not recognizing you, your grace."

Stapleton chuckled. "You thought I was talking out of turn, obviously."

"Yes," Jeremy assured him quickly. "I would never had spoken to you that way if—"

The duke cut him off. "She's impossible, that daughter of mine. Takes after her mother in that respect. Well, it was fun while it lasted, but I suppose introductions must be made. Nicolas Westfall, Duke of Stapleton. Father of the exquisite Lady Fanny Rivers. A woman whose honor you defended admirably, I must say, with so little provocation."

Jeremy bowed again, face flaming still. "A pleasure, and I am sorry for the lack of respect when I spoke to you. I should never have…"

"Spoken your mind? Of course, you should

have leaped to my daughter's defense. I did my best to bait you, after all. I assume Fenton was similarly rude. My idea but I'm sure he went along with my request with great enthusiasm. My daughter has told me all about her *increased interest in the theater*, and while I disapprove of her habit of taking in strays, I am prepared to make allowances during your stay for the sake of peace. But be aware that your time among us is limited." The duke strolled to the door as he continued, "You will be subjected to worse interviews when the family gathers together again. Dinner will be served at seven o'clock. I'll send a servant to fetch you, so you don't lose your way. Wear the navy-blue wool Weston tonight."

When the door swung shut behind him, there was silence for a moment before the servants burst out laughing again. "At least you didn't ask him to stir the coals like Lady Rivers' last stray did," one said.

Jeremy glared at the men around him. "Does he do that to all his daughter's new acquaintances?"

"Oh, frequently. Says he can judge a character better if they think he's ordinary." They all tugged on their forelocks, grinning. "Happy to be of service to you, Mr. Dawes. If there's anything you need, just ring the bell beside the fire."

Jeremy shut his eyes as they filed out. He had imagined the Duke of Stapleton as a remote, grandiose man who would look down his nose at those he considered beneath him—which should have been everyone. Jeremy had actually been dreading the introduction. Lady Rivers had promised Jeremy would be welcomed at Stapleton, but he had never imagined the duke would be the one to show him to his room...or out-act him in his first scene.

Chapter Three

Fanny hurried toward the east sitting room, skirting around other guests in her father's home, keen to be reunited with Jeremy Dawes. She had returned too late last night to find him still awake, but she had enquired about him and been assured he had been given every consideration for his comfort. He had even dined with her father, who had not attended Lord Rafferty's home due to some sort of emergency on the estate.

"Lady Rivers!"

"I cannot stop," she protested, one finger raised toward Lady Eastwick, who was a dear friend. "I am late for a very important meeting."

Fanny hurried on, knowing curiosity would be stirred by her unseemly haste. What better way to stir interest than to be seen rushing to meet a young man?

In the hall outside the manor's smallest sitting room, she paused, took a steadying breath, and smoothed her hair. She was strangely nervous, or perhaps excited was a correct term. She was about to embark on a bit of deception that would guarantee she remained undistracted for the next two weeks.

Fanny knocked and then slipped into the sitting room where Jeremy was supposed to be. A stranger with dark short-cropped hair stood before the window with his back to her. "Oh, I am so sorry," she murmured, apologizing for blundering into the wrong chamber.

"Lady Rivers?"

She turned back as she recognized the voice. "Jeremy?"

"In the flesh," he promised, spreading his arms wide and grinning.

Fanny managed to close her mouth with some effort and pushed the door closed behind her. She stared at him, more astonished with every step she took in his direction. He was almost unrecognizable from when she'd last laid eyes on him. If not for the green of his eyes surrounded by long lashes and the flirtatious quirk of his lips, she might never believe they'd ever met. "What happened to you?"

His smile faded and he glanced down at his attire. "Weston, Lock, and Hoby, and the valet you sent to dress me every day, I suppose." He raked his hand over his shorn head. "Was I wrong to heed to their suggestions?"

"No," she hastily assured him, moving for a closer inspection. He was the same height, only now he appeared much more muscular. And now that his exceedingly long dark hair had been trimmed away from his face, he seemed a completely changed man. Older, more self-assured. The difference in his presence was remarkable, and it might take her a while to grow accustomed to the change herself. She'd thought him pleasing to look at before, but now…well…ladies would swoon.

He absolutely looked the part of a gentleman of the *ton*. "You look exactly right to me."

"I'm glad. For a moment I was afraid you were unhappy."

"No indeed." She prowled around him, inspecting him from head to toe. The perfectly fitted Weston coat accentuated his wide shoulders and the rest revealed his trim physique. She bit her lip, liking what she saw very much. "Thank you for coming."

"Of course," he said and then offered a courtly bow. "Lady Rivers, you are as ever the most radiant woman in all of England."

She extended her hands, blushing at his words. "Mr. Dawes, always such a flatterer."

"Not a word I say is untrue," he promised.

Fanny steadied her smile. She was as susceptible to flattery as the next woman. But she was his patroness first and they had business to discuss before her play began. "Won't you sit and talk with me."

"Until the end of time," he promised with a teasing smile.

The first time they'd met had been at the theater. She'd not been there to meet him but another, more popular actor who had asked for an introduction. The actor had turned out to be arrogant and far less interesting than the understudy's understudy, lurking in the shadows and mimicking the man she was speaking to. Jeremy, once she'd dismissed the leading man, had come up and started flattering her outrageously, making her blush and laugh while he juggled pork pies for her amusement and made them disappear.

To this day, she'd no idea what he'd done with them.

Fanny considered herself a good judge of character. Jeremy Dawes had interested her from the start and still did. She had watched for him in later performances, and she'd quickly decided to champion his ambitions for bigger roles. And when a more pressing need had arisen outside the theater, Jeremy had been easily won over to her cause.

She gestured to a pair of elegant chairs nearby and seated herself. "Did you have a comfortable journey, sir?"

Jeremy Dawes flicked out the tails of his coat before slowly lowering himself to the edge of his like any well-bred man might. "As well as one can on the mail coach, I expect." He sounded so proper now, compared to the way he'd once spoken when he'd been acting the part of a sour, grumbling merchant. He reached down beside the chair and presented her with a leather satchel. "This is yours, I believe."

"Oh, thank you. I cannot imagine why I left this behind." Fanny quickly checked the contents were as she remembered—papers relating to a recent acquisition. All seemed in order, and she closed the clasp again. "Have you eaten today?"

Jeremy grinned. "Always thinking about my stomach, my lady. Yes, I have. A servant brought a tray to my room with the duke's compliments. I was very disappointed there wasn't a single pork pie to be seen, though."

"My father doesn't know about your passion for a pork pie, though I am glad he's taken an interest in you. That will help solidify your reason for being here. He was quite surprised by our arrangement."

Jeremy shrugged. "I'll give him no reason to regret my coming."

"Good. I will make sure you are introduced to everyone as soon as possible, and then we can go on as…"

"Sweethearts? Would-be lovers?" Jeremy's grin spread slowly on his face as Fanny blushed anew. "I must admit I'm looking forward to expanding my part as far as it can go, my lady. But I do have a few questions."

"I'll answer if I can."

"May I occasionally forget the formalities and refer to you by your given name? I think it will more easily convey our growing familiarity than any overt physical contact. Not immediately, of course. We shouldn't beat our audience over the head with the suggestion."

"I suppose you could, provided the situation calls for such intimacy between us."

"Good." He leaned close. "Where shall we begin?"

"With introductions, but unfortunately they will have to wait. I have a pressing need to make a call to a neighbor's home this morning."

"Might I have the honor of escorting you?"

"Why not? We can continue our conversation on the way there." She stopped to look at him. "Oh, had you made any plans for the day yet?"

He shook his head. "I have no intention of making plans without speaking to you first for the next two weeks."

He'd promised he was all hers to direct for the next few weeks. A boon no other man had ever given her so easily. "I had so wanted to see you last night, but I returned so late. You must have been very tired from your journey."

"You could have woken me. I wouldn't have objected."

"That might have been too obvious, and I don't want everyone thinking that I lack sense."

"Nor do I."

"It is one thing to seem involved without providing proof that we might be."

"Well, I am available for any scene you deem necessary."

Fanny let her eyes drift over him again. There

was far too much to admire now in that handsome package. He was just here to flirt with her and seem like they might be involved. "Thank you. Are you ready to go with me now?"

"Indeed. I already have my new hat waiting over there for just such an excursion." Jeremy stood, collected his hat, and carefully fitted it to his head. He extended his hand to Fanny when done. "My lady."

She smiled and collected her bonnet and shawl, too. Jeremy helped her don the shawl, his fingers lightly brushing her shoulder.

She looked back at him. "I must say the time you've dedicated to your role has been time well spent. Your manner of speaking and poise are exactly right for the setting. Do you agree?"

"I am sure the gentlemen I've studied as inspiration for my role would have found at least three things wrong with my performance."

"They'll never know," she promised. Fanny had invited several male friends to a dinner one night and had asked Jeremy to pose as a servant to observe them in action. He'd said the conversation at port had been rather coarse, but the rest had been worthwhile viewing.

They stepped outside into the bright sunshine and immediately heard screaming. Fanny sighed. "My nephews are at it again."

"I am surprised they're not shut up in the nursery," Jeremy murmured quietly.

"T'would be impossible to keep them locked

in given their adventurous natures." Fanny's nephews might be described as mischievous by those outside the family. The family knew better. The pair were the devil's spawn. Angelic of face but possessed with inexhaustible imaginations. "You'll likely see them everywhere. Come quickly before they see me and try to follow us."

The journey to the Hawthorne estate was a pleasant stroll when one did not hurry, and Fanny slowed their steps once they reached the safety of the trees, well beyond the sight of Stapleton Manor's many windows.

"Who are you going to see?"

"Mr. and Mrs. Hawthorne. Neighbors on the other side of these woods."

"Wonderful." He looked at her, frowning. "We need to talk about how we greet each other, too."

"I don't understand."

"To play the part of a smitten lady, you'll need to behave a certain way. Do you remember your favorite performances at the theater where characters first meet each other?"

"A few," she said.

"When you appear in a room, I will most likely try to catch your eye. The degree of welcome in your response will need to grow as time passes. But too much enthusiasm at first will seem false. The danger will be in allowing our enthusiasm to spoil the performance. Usually it's worked out during rehearsals, but we have little time for that I suspect. Let me show you."

He took up her hand, raised it and lifted his shoulders as he declared gushingly, "My lady, it has been too long."

Fanny giggled.

"See? Utterly false." He repositioned himself a few yards away. "Now this…"

He met her gaze and a soft smile turned up his lips. His steps were unhurried as he crossed to her a second time, and he never looked away. "My dear lady, it has been too long." He caught her outstretched hand and the degree of warmth in his smile increased a little. "Now you respond," he whispered out the side of his mouth.

"Oh, yes," Fanny replied, doing her best to come up with something suitable. "Mr. Dawes, how I have missed you, sir," she promised, doing her best to mimic the inflections of a lovestruck woman.

"A little too strong, perhaps," he suggested. "Remember we're not trying to beat them over the head with the suspicion. A hint of partiality is all we need to make it seem a romance is in the air."

He brought her hand to his lips. Although it might seem so to anyone observing them, his lips never once touched her gloves. He raised his eyes to her and winked.

Fanny fought a blush.

He dropped her hand without kissing it. "Now that was a well-played scene, I should think. A pity there were no witnesses."

Fanny nodded, suddenly aware of the warmth

of her cheeks and the rapid beat of her heart. She dropped her gaze from his. "There should be at least one next time."

"And one is all we need to begin a suspicion." He held out his arm to her. "Shall we continue?"

"Indeed."

He looked down on her with a cheeky smile. "London was quiet without you."

She looked up at him concerned. "Was there still no word when the new play will begin rehearsals?"

"None," he promised. "And I am grateful, too, because I will have more time and energy to devote to you. I promise to put all my effort into making this performance as realistic as possible and not being an embarrassment."

"Mr. Dawes, I could never be embarrassed by you."

"Thank you. I do hope you're right."

She smiled at the young actor by her side, encouraging him, she hoped, to be more optimistic. Her play would be a success in her eyes if the fortune hunters left her alone, and if it didn't exactly turn out as planned, she'd make adjustments accordingly.

Every now and then a beam of light would strike him, revealing the odd copper strand in his hair. He was quite dashing now. But Jeremy didn't need training in turning a woman's head. He had an agile tongue for flattery which was so useful in society. "You *do* look the part, and sound it to my ear."

"I'll consider that the highest compliment of my life," he promised placing his free hand over his heart.

Fanny laughed, clinging to his arm. The man was outrageous.

They strolled along side by side, Mr. Dawes peppering her with questions about the family and her childhood home. But he was constantly looking about them. "Is something wrong?"

"It's eerie under so many trees."

"I've always thought trees romantic. I had my first kiss in these very woods," she admitted with a laugh.

Jeremy looked at her with one brow raised high. "May I ask who the lucky man was? Or was it your late husband?"

"A lady never tells," she said with a coy smile.

"Not your husband then," he guessed, correctly too. "So is the fellow at liberty still, or did your father lock him in his dungeon for his daring?"

Fanny laughed. What would he say if he knew Fanny had been the one to take liberties? People always assumed she had been a good girl, which was a mistake on their part, really. "My father isn't a tyrant, and he doesn't have a dungeon, either. Papa never knew about that kiss and he never will."

"Ha! So you were kissed by a scoundrel, and he got away with it. Lucky devil."

"I suppose," she murmured. "I am actually

very glad I never had to marry him. Scoundrels make terrible husbands in my opinion."

"And that is the only opinion that matters today," he promised.

She looked at him curiously. "So, where did your first kiss take place, Mr. Dawes?"

"Oh, no. I'm an innocent still," he promised with a sly wink. "Never been kissed."

Fanny laughed outright at his boast. "By all means, keep your own counsel. I don't mean to pry."

Jeremy's grin widened. "Yes, you do, my lady. You've been prying into my past since the day we met."

"It's your own fault for being so mysterious," she complained.

He looked ahead. "There's nothing about my past that a proper lady needs to hear."

Fanny disagreed, but Jeremy was stubborn about certain things. It had taken her a month to find out he lacked any family or home other than the theater.

They finally came to a trickling brook with stepping-stones across it. It was a pretty hidden spot deep in the woods. "Here we are."

Mr. Dawes looked around, his eyes narrowing. "Is this where your infamous first kiss was stolen?"

"Enjoyed, and yes, I was on my way back from a party and got a stone in my slipper. I had to stop to remove it and had lagged behind."

"And the scoundrel took advantage of your lack of chaperone."

She couldn't continue to lie when the truth was more fun. She shook her head. "It was I who took advantage of him."

Jeremy Dawes blinked but then his eyes lit up with delight. "*You* did?"

She shrugged. "I was a precocious sixteen-year-old and determined to get my first kiss before my young sisters did. When it was over, I felt decidedly smug for weeks."

Ordinarily she wouldn't confide her past conquests to anyone. However, she had a part to play and becoming comfortable with each other would help their performances. She was a smitten lady from today. Walking along with a handsome man she admired. Tongues were meant to wag enough when they were seen together so that her real would-be suitors would think twice before interrupting.

Jeremy shook his head. "My first was with a whore."

Fanny winced. First kiss or sexual encounter? He didn't clarify further, and Fanny wouldn't ask. She suspected they might very well be the same for a man of his background. But she felt bad for him. He did not sound as if his first kiss was as happy a memory as hers had always been.

"I knew you'd be repulsed."

She lay a hand on his arm. They were very different, but she would not let that taint her opinion of him. "Mr. Dawes, I do not intend for one moment to criticize you, but I regret the encounter for the obvious lack of affection in your voice when you spoke of the experience." She studied him a moment and then, since they were alone, stretched up on her toes to kiss him on the cheek.

He smiled shyly. "That wasn't bad, but I think you could do better."

"Oh," Fanny complained as she swatted him with her hand. "Are you going to now coach me on kissing, too?"

"Kissing in front of an audience is different than real kissing," he informed her. He drew close, catching hold of her hand, holding it against his chest. His face lowered until he was an inch away from her lips. He stopped there, his brown eyes warming her all over. "It's more convincing if the kiss could happen but doesn't."

She looked up into his eyes, waiting to be kissed, and when his gaze flickered to her lips, she almost couldn't breathe for the anticipation curling through her. "Jeremy."

"Fanny, darling," he said with a sigh, but suddenly took a pace back and let go her hand. "Like that."

The disappointment Fanny felt was unbelievable. She'd imagined he'd kiss her, but it was all an act. The spell was broken. The scene over.

Fanny took a swipe at his arm again for leading

her on but then laughed along with him. It was just a game. "You are horribly believable."

"If only the company could see me now. I'd be guaranteed a leading role with you playing opposite." Jeremy put his hands behind his back. "There's something of a long walk still to go, isn't there?"

Fanny put her hand to her belly, realizing her stomach was still doing little flips of disappointment over that pretend almost-kiss. "Yes, and we should be going so we might return in time for luncheon with everyone. I'll introduce you to everyone then."

They moved off again, and Fanny struggled to find a new topic to talk about, other than return to discussing their past amours and their current play.

Mr. Dawes gallantly held her hand when they encountered tree roots that had made the footpath uneven. He helped her cross and then let her go. "When did you meet Lord Rivers?"

"A few years after my first kiss. He was much better than the scoundrel and had much to teach me about passion."

Jeremy laughed softly. "I'm beginning to suspect he'd little to teach you about passion but the mechanics of coupling."

How right he was. By the time Fanny had married, she'd devoured every salacious word written about intimacy and gossiped with friends, married or not, about their romantic encounters. She had been well prepared for taking a husband the first time. She might look and sound like a proper lady, but her mind was decidedly wicked. "Mr. Dawes, there is another delicate discussion we must have before you are introduced to the wedding guests."

"Oh?"

"Yes, and it is a little uncomfortable discussion to have, I'm afraid. Should you encounter a lady you fancy, do tell me, and be discreet if you arrange a private meeting with them."

His eyes had widened as she'd spoken, and she charged on.

"Gentlemen and women of the *ton* have a tendency to hop beds at house parties, and while not discouraged, it can have dire consequences. Married ladies possess a degree of boredom with their husbands, many think the rules no longer apply once they've fulfilled their duty of delivering a healthy heir and spare. All handsome gentlemen, wealthy or not, married or not, are generally considered fair game. I wouldn't want you to find yourself involved in a scandal, unaware of the danger or consequences."

He nodded. "Do you mean the consequences of being cited in divorce proceedings?"

"I was more worried about you having to meet a husband at dawn for a duel of honor," she whispered.

He laughed. "I hadn't planned to kiss any married women. Or any at all."

A degree of relief and disappointment swept

through her. "According to my younger brother, no one ever does until an opportunity presents itself."

"Your brother, Lord Samuel Westfall?"

"Yes, he is something of a libertine, I am afraid. Half my friends think themselves in love with him."

"He loves but never offers marriage. Why? Does he keep a mistress?"

Fanny felt a pang of discomfort at the question but in his role as her sweetheart, Jeremy might find himself in a situation where he was expected to know certain personal details about members of her family. "Not that I know of. He was married once but she died, and he never got over the loss. I miss Gabriella very much still, too. She was a fine woman and a good sister."

Jeremy Dawes nodded slowly, watching her. "They say weddings bring happiness and melancholy. That's why so many plays feature them."

"Indeed, they do." They reached the edge of the wood and stopped to admire the view of the Hawthorne estate from the boundary gateway. Fanny searched the distance and sighed. The pretty estate home and outbuildings had lost none of their charms since her last visit. Although…

She squinted at the land and buildings again, noticing the early signs of neglect perhaps. "The Hawthornes haven't the same funds as my family. But they are good people. I heard a rumor yesterday all was not well, though. I see, problems here already. Some neglect."

Jeremy looked at her quickly, and then the weed choked orchard. "I'll hope that is not true."

"So do I, Jeremy. So do I," she whispered.

Chapter Four

Jeremy stood back as Lady Rivers greeted a tired old woman in a faded sitting room. "My dear, I would have come sooner had I known the news was so grim."

Mrs. Hawthorne's eyes welled with tears. "I did not want to believe I could lose him," she whispered. "Not like this. Not yet. The children need their father. What will we do without him?"

Lady Rivers held Mrs. Hawthorne by the hand. "Antony is the best of men, and it is my hope he might pull through yet. We must have faith."

Mrs. Hawthorne appeared not to have slept for a week or more. Her eyes were puffy, perhaps from crying, and there were deep grooves of sorrow etched on her face. Although he was glad to view such a sorrow-filled scene, Jeremy wished he had waited outside.

Unfortunately, Lady Rivers' words only brought the woman closer to the brink of tears. Losing a husband and father must be difficult. Jeremy had never known his parents, or if he had, he couldn't remember them now.

Mrs. Hawthorne seemed to calm slowly, but then she glanced toward Jeremy with an apologetic smile, as if just remembering he was standing there listening to her weep. She wiped her tears away. "I don't believe we've been introduced."

Fanny smiled and gestured Jeremy closer. "My dear, this is Mr. Jeremy Dawes, my new London friend. He's an actor and he'll be joining us for my sister's wedding."

The woman mumbled a greeting of welcome. "Oh, yes, the wedding. An event sure to be a source of conversation for many years to come. I was very sorry to have missed your father's wedding to dear Gillian, and yours, too. Now I could miss this one as well."

"My wedding was many years ago," Lady Rivers murmured.

"You were so beautiful," Mrs. Hawthorne claimed.

"I was then."

In Jeremy's opinion, Lady Rivers was beautiful now. She had such vitality and a wonderful habit of laughing at almost everything he said. There were a handful of years' difference in their ages, with Jeremy being younger, if he was right about his own age.

Mrs. Hawthorne dabbed at her eyes. "Perhaps I'll be lucky and attend the next wedding. Yours perhaps."

Fanny shook her head. "I shall never marry again. You know that."

Mrs. Hawthorne sighed. "Not even for love?"

She laughed softly. "Especially not then. Love

would suit me very ill. I'm enjoying life far too much on my own."

"It suits me very well." Mrs. Hawthorne sniffed. "I can't bear to think of a world without my Antony."

Fanny was suddenly hugging the woman, but Jeremy heard her whisper, "If I could survive losing Rivers, you can, too."

And then Mrs. Hawthorne fell apart completely, sobbing her eyes out.

When Lady Rivers continued to hold the weeping woman, Jeremy began edging backward toward the door. This is where the scene should naturally end if it were a play. There was little he could do or say to be a comfort to a woman about to lose the love of her life. Everyone died, whether you loved them or not.

Jeremy had reached the doorway when Fanny noticed his intention was to go. "Thank you," she mouthed, her arms still about the sobbing woman.

He retraced his steps toward the front door, uncertain of what to do with himself now though. But he would wait, of course, for when Lady Rivers had need of him again.

Before he reached the peace of the outdoors, however, he heard a sound.

A whisper quickly silenced. A whimper or a sob.

A young child.

Jeremy looked about for the source and found five sets of sad eyes watching him from a window seat in the nearest room. Fanny had only mentioned there was a daughter of marriageable age, not that there were a handful of tiny ones, too. They looked to be of an age to walk and talk but sat alone, with not a servant anywhere in sight to look after them. Their sad faces tugged at his heart.

He stepped cautiously into the room and lowered himself to their level. "Good morning."

But they just watched him.

The children wore smocks and had their hair cut to a length just below their ears. It was impossible to tell boy from girl given the way they were dressed. They were probably too young to understand the scope of the loss that was about to befall the family, but they were sad just the same. "You'll be all right if you look after each other, I promise," he said, hoping that could be true. "What are your names?"

"They've been told to be quiet," a woman said suddenly behind him. "And not talk to strangers."

Jeremy shot to his feet and faced a woman of an age to be out. Despite the glare, she appeared worn down in spirit and resembled Mrs. Hawthorne a great deal. This could only be the daughter of marriageable age he'd heard about. "You must be Miss Hawthorne."

She did nothing to confirm nor deny. "Who are you?"

"Mr. Dawes. I am Lady Rivers' good friend. You must not have seen her arrival on foot from the woods."

"No. I was taking a walk in the opposite direction," she said slowly, but still seemed skeptical.

"Lady Rivers and your mother are just down the hall in the sitting room."

Miss Hawthorne looked down the hall and then back at him, her eyes full of suspicion.

Jeremy put his hands behind his back. If he'd intended to steal anything from this house, he had sufficient time already to have made an escape. "I promise not to move from this spot until you confirm it."

She frowned and then rushed down the hallway. At the sitting-room door, she cried out and rushed inside. The children followed after their older sister. Jeremy could imagine an affectionate greeting being exchanged within the sitting room, but he stayed rooted to the spot until Miss Hawthorne reappeared again and released him from his promise.

"Lady Rivers asked me to remind you not to go too far."

He nodded. "I had only intended to stroll the gardens closest to the house."

She glanced back inside the sitting room, a frown growing. "She said that would be best."

As he turned, he noticed the children again. His character, if serious about courting Lady Rivers, would certainly try to win over her friends and be helpful. "Would you allow me to take the children outside for some air and exercise? Just in the gardens. They have been very quiet, and I think it would cheer them up to be in the sunshine."

Miss Hawthorne seemed to sag at his offer. "It has been very hard to entertain them."

"Then please allow me to be of assistance. Perhaps the children can show me their favorite play spots outside."

"I think they would like that."

Another quick grin, and Jeremy held out a hand to the young ones. "Shall we go outside and see if we can find any pretty flowers to brighten your mother's sitting room?"

They rushed outside, ignoring his outstretched hand but holding on to each other. Jeremy followed, watching them run around through the gardens, then stop to confer with each other at a whisper. Then suddenly they darted off toward a distant garden gate.

"Wait! Please not too far," he called but was ignored.

Jeremy lengthened his stride and gave chase into what seemed to be an orchard, annoyed that those seemingly placid children were as wily as any overly ambitious understudy determined to steal the scene. He eventually found them all sitting beneath an apple tree, holding hands and whispering.

He counted heads to make sure he had them all.

Then countered again—because he had two

more heads than he'd thought he'd started out with.

But then he shrugged. Lady Rivers hadn't said how many in number the Hawthornes were. He had seven now, instead of the five he started with. That could be all of them or perhaps there were more still somewhere about the estate.

They didn't seem to need him to entertain them, so he leaned against an old apple tree, a silent observer. Jeremy looked about him and reached up to brush an apple hanging above his head. He wasn't hungry, and so he left it there to finish growing. But before Lady Rivers and her money had come into his life, he wouldn't have hesitated to take what he needed to survive.

He was well versed in criminal activities, though Lady Rivers had no idea of his past. And she never would if he had his way. To her, his life began and ended at the theater. He would lose her patronage if she learned his first profession had been thief...and that he'd been rather too good at it.

He looked about again, taking in his surroundings. What a world to grow up in. No filth, abundant food just waiting to be picked and eaten from any tree or vine. This family was luckier than any he'd ever known. They would have every opportunity in life.

He became aware that the whispers continued, and glances in his direction grew in number, then the children were all up on their feet again. They tore through the garden, running away from him, gathering up flowers, a little from each plant, and once they had enough, they ran off together again.

Jeremy was forced to give chase, and he was glad their haste seemed to be a return to the Hawthorne house only.

He caught up to them just as they started up the stairs.

But then they began to creep, tiptoeing through the doorway into the dim inner hall. Jeremy followed in a similar fashion, as silent as he'd been when stealing his way into a stranger's home, because he sensed a change in the air inside the house. Years of watching others and listening to his instincts told him all was not well.

Down the hall, servants had gathered together, faces lowered. Fingers covering their lips.

And in the room they stood outside of, a woman suddenly began to wail, desperately sad.

Heartbroken.

Jeremy froze as the horrible sound of loss faded away, only to start up again.

If he was not mistaken, the gentleman of the house had just passed away.

Jeremy lowered his head and sent up a brief prayer for the man's soul. But two of the boys ushered the others down the hall, headed toward that far room.

Jeremy hesitated to follow but decided he should, in case he was asked to take them away again.

He reached the doorway and spotted the Hawthornes hugging each other beside a large bed.

Lady Rivers was nearby, her back pressed to the wall, silent tears streaming down her cheeks in grief.

He went to her side, and when he whispered her given name, she turned into his shoulder immediately and began to sob her heart out. Surprised by her grief, he gently put his arm around her, and held her close.

While he held her, he looked about the room, a man's bedchamber, where a still form lie, eyes closed.

Unmoving.

This was not the first corpse Jeremy had looked upon in his short life. He'd seen bodies in terrible condition in London's filthy streets and homes, pulled from the alley behind the theater, too. Vagrants and victims of murder or neglect.

Mr. Hawthorne must have only died moments ago, but it was clear to see he was terribly missed already by the family.

Family. Jeremy had little experience with that. He had the theater but that simply wasn't the same.

Finally, Lady Rivers remembered herself and drew back and gave Jeremy a tremulous smile. She patted her cheeks, wiping away tears. "I have known him all my life."

Jeremy nodded. "He was a lucky man then."

Her answering smile wobbled. "My father

must be informed. I need to find a servant to break the news to him gently. They were great friends, but he'd wanted his illness kept a secret."

What servants he could see were all weeping in the hall, and Jeremy felt they shouldn't be asked to abandon their mistress at such a time. Jeremy didn't want to leave Lady Rivers, but he also didn't *need* to stay. "I can do that for you. I can tell him."

Lady Rivers took hold of his hand and squeezed. She looked at him with such gratitude, he felt ten feet tall suddenly. "That would be very much appreciated, Mr. Dawes. Let him know he passed quietly, without any pain."

"I will," he promised.

She turned away, facing the elder Miss Hawthorne. "Boys, you two should return to your father."

Jeremy stared at the two children trying to hide their faces. "Are they not Mrs. Hawthorne's children?"

"No, these are my brother's twins. They'll show you the way home. They know the path very well."

The twins whispered to each other and slid from Miss Hawthorne's lap. Then they started placing flowers around the late Mr. Hawthorne's body, and Jeremy sucked in a breath to fight a wave of unexpected emotion.

Unfortunately, Mrs. Hawthorne saw what they had done and began to weep violently again.

"Oh, my dear boys," Fanny whispered, patting

away her own tears. "They did that for their mother, too."

"I can find my own way," he quickly assured her, feeling unexpectedly emotional about the loss of a man he'd never know and a pressing need to escape the feeling.

Lady Rivers drew him from the room and wiped at her eyes with a whisp of fine embroidered linen that passed for a handkerchief as they headed down the hall. "I had forgotten how much it hurts to lose someone you love. I haven't had reason to cry since…"

"Since you lost Lord Rivers?" he answered for her.

She nodded. "It was sudden with him. I had no warning. No time to prepare myself. I didn't know what to do when I suddenly lost the love of my life."

"Were you alone?"

"Yes. My father and sisters were here."

Lady Rivers suddenly shook her head and patted at her cheeks again. "Look at me. Falling to pieces and boring you with the dim and distant past."

"I'm never bored when I'm near you," he promised, and it was true. He touched her arm lightly. "Can I bring anything back with me? A handkerchief…your youngest sister, perhaps?"

"Jessica will undoubtedly come as soon as she hears the news, but I might need a fresh handkerchief."

He dug in his coat pocket and presented his pristine white handkerchief to her. "In case you need another before I return with your own."

She held it tightly and nodded. "Thank you."

"I'll return soon." And he finally turned away, eager to go so he could return again.

Lady Rivers followed him a few steps. "Always remember to take the right fork all the way home to Stapleton."

"The right," Jeremy repeated, grateful for that piece of advice since he'd simply been following Lady Rivers' lead on the way here. "I'll return as soon as I've notified the duke."

"Thank you, but I will be here for quite some time."

He didn't doubt Mrs. Hawthorne would appreciate her company and support. "I'll wait for you for as long as it takes."

Chapter Five

"It's been a long day," Fanny murmured to herself as the carriage rolled along the Stapleton drive around midnight. She had stayed with Mrs. Hawthorne as her father had said his goodbyes to a lifelong friend. But it was clear her father was deeply affected. He seemed to be in something of a daze. Gillian had hold of Father's hand, talking quietly to him. Mentioning when the babe kicked in a bid to cheer him up. But not even the antics of his next child seemed to cheer him for very long.

But that was the way it went when someone you cared about was around no more. The world seemed a little less real, less bright for a while. It had for her.

Fanny wet her lips and glanced sideways. Jeremy Dawes seemed to be dozing as they rolled along in her father's carriage. He'd been such a help and support during the evening. She was humbled by his compassion. For the Hawthornes and for her, as well. There had been many occasions when a look from him, the brush of his hand, had brought Fanny back from the brink of tears. He'd kept to the background, listening and offering a quiet word whenever she'd needed the distraction of his conversation.

And that had been often, she'd found.

Fanny put her head back against the squabs and sighed. It had been a terrible day for her. She had been reminded too often of the day her late husband had passed away so many years ago that her heart hurt again. She'd had no family to support her then, and she'd made few close friends in the neighborhood around her husband's estate. It was why, since Rivers had passed, Fanny spent so little time there anymore.

Too many memories, too many regrets for what should have a been a long and happy marriage cut tragically short.

But Mrs. Hawthorne had friends by her side. Children who needed her. She couldn't stop weeping over the loss of her husband, but she had many shoulders to cry on in the coming days and years. She would not be alone or forgotten. Father had already mentioned he could take over the running of the fields and livestock on her behalf until the Hawthornes' only boy was old enough to shoulder the responsibility.

Jeremy moved, brushing against her shoulder as they turned down the drive, and when she glanced his way, another smile played over his lips. She sought out his hand, seeking his comfort and strength in the dark. They were almost home and soon they would separate.

She would have to stand on her own two feet then and be composed. But she was far from it.

She'd rather curl up in a ball and cry than see anybody.

When the carriage stopped before Stapleton, her father roused and helped his heavily pregnant wife out. Jeremy exited next and held his hand out to Fanny to take. She was grateful for that hand because she was not feeling at all steady. He hooked her arm through his and escorted her inside, following Father and Gillian silently.

"Your family requests a word with you, your grace," the butler murmured as soon as they entered the hall.

Father waved him away. "Not tonight. I'll speak with everyone in the morning."

Father curled his arm around Gillian as they ascended the staircase together, guided by a servant carrying a brace of candles. "Good night, Father. Good night Gillian," Fanny called.

Only Gillian waved and then they disappeared from sight.

Fanny drew in a breath and turned to the butler. "Where is everyone?"

"Waiting in the library, my lady."

She nodded. "I'll speak with them for my father. Why don't you turn in. There's nothing more to be done tonight that can't wait until tomorrow."

"I was just about to arrange the delivery of tea to the duke and duchess' chambers," the butler promised.

"Thank you."

"If there's anything you need, my lady, just ring," he murmured.

Fanny turned for the library and let herself in, aware that Jeremy had followed her without being asked.

Her brother's jumped to their feet and rushed over to embrace her. Milo caught her face between his hands and stared into her eyes. "So it is true?"

"Yes. It was a peaceful passing."

Milo hugged her tightly, and then Samuel did as well. "You could have sent for either one of us. We would have come at a run."

Fanny shrugged. "I wasn't alone. I had Mr. Dawes, and the twins were there for a time, until Father ordered them home. Whitfield and Jessica will spend the night there tonight."

Milo noticed Jeremy and nodded. "Thank you for staying with my sister."

"No thanks are necessary."

Fanny cleared her throat. "Papa and Gillian have retired for the night already. As you might imagine, Papa is quite upset. Tomorrow, he'll let us know the plans for the funeral and for observing mourning."

Milo nodded. "I've already decided to stay on for longer than I'd planned, keep his spirits up."

"I'll be staying, too," Samuel added. "The twins are always a good distraction and with the duchess due soon, and him fretting all the time over her, I think it is doubly important to stay."

They all looked at Fanny, but she had made no

similar decision. She hadn't even considered what happened after the wedding, if there would still be one. "You should head for bed."

"What about you?"

"I am for bed, too, shortly."

Milo kissed her brow. "Don't stay up too long."

"Wake me if you find you cannot sleep," Samuel offered.

The pair filed out, leaving Jeremy and Fanny alone in the library. She loved her papa's library, but women were not really allowed to linger without his permission. She remembered spying on him reading here when she'd been a girl. He'd always known when he was being watched and used to let her come in if she promised to be very quiet.

Jeremy began putting out the candles, circling the room until only one remained burning on a table beside Fanny. He paused and then slowly doused it, too.

Fanny reached for him and found herself enfolded in Jeremy's arms once more. There was a gentle strength about him that she found entirely comforting. His heart beat steadily under her cheek, soothing her. She wished she could stay like this forever. But no one stayed forever.

She drew back from him.

"Time for bed for you, too," he suggested in a whisper.

"Yes, bed."

Her bed, alone, where she would imagine the

day over and over again and probably not sleep a wink.

Jeremy's fingers twined with hers and he pulled her toward the hall. Fanny followed his lead, through the silent house, up the grand staircase.

At the top, she paused. "You're very sure-footed in the dark."

"Candles cost money," he whispered. "And when you don't have it to buy them, you learn to navigate without."

Fanny turned for her chambers and the privacy they would afford her. She was teary again, something she'd rather no one else see.

"Are you all right, my lady?" Jeremy asked as he followed after her a few steps.

Fanny wasn't sure. She had liked Antony Hawthorne very much, but surely she had not admired him *this* much. How could she explain her feelings when she really didn't understand them herself? "No. Not really."

The man drew closer. "What can I do to make you feel better?"

Fanny bowed her head. "What can anyone do to make the pain of loss go away or lessen."

He placed his hands on her arms. "Rest will do you the world of good."

But she didn't think she could sleep without seeing Hawthorne's face and that of her own late husband in death. "I will try."

Jeremy inched closer still, and then leaned past

her to open her bedchamber door. "Good night, my lady. I wish you only good dreams."

As he said the last, she inhaled deeply. The scent of Jeremy so close, the warmth of his hand on her arm, made her breath stall. She remembered him holding her that day, beside the bed of the late Mr. Hawthorne, and downstairs in Father's library just now. It had felt good to be comforted by him. She thought it would feel good again now, too.

Fanny reached blindly for his hand and, once caught, she drew him into the bedchamber with her. The door shut with a soft click and then she was in his arms, though she hadn't had to ask to be held by him yet again.

His long arms wrapped around her body tightly, his warm hand pressed against the back of her neck. He dipped his head low beside hers and the warmth of his breath against her ear made her feel infinitely better. Fanny pressed herself tight against Jeremy and let him soothe her in a way she'd never imagined she'd ever need.

Of all the men in the world, an actor, a man she paid to appear as her admirer, was exactly what she needed most tonight. She turned her head so her cheek rested nearer his heart. The steady thumping rhythm made her warm all over again and pushed back the ugly memories of death.

She held on to him as long as she dared and then drew back. "I'm sorry, I don't know what has come over me today."

"Everyone needs somebody now and then," he murmured in a voice gone deeper and husky. *Intimate.* He remained close. "May I ask you a personal question?"

"Of course."

"How, where, did your husband die?"

Fanny gulped and closed her eyes. The most painful memory of all assailed her and it took a moment to form an answer. "He died in bed next to me. I woke and turned to wake him with a kiss and… I never want to live through a moment like that again."

He frowned. "Is that why you haven't remarried?"

"No. Yes, perhaps it is one of the reasons."

He winced. "I'm sorry there was no one to comfort you then."

Fanny nodded. "There were servants about, but it's not the same as having someone, family, who loves you unconditionally to cling to at such a time."

"I'm sure it's not." Jeremy smiled quickly. "It's clear your family love you very much."

"And there's nothing I wouldn't do for them."

She imagined him nodding because she could still hardly see.

"Well, I should go before I'm discovered where I ought not to be found."

But she needed him still. She didn't want to spend the night on her own.

Fanny wet her lips and looked up at him. Her

arrangement with Jeremy had never been about having a true friendship, but that didn't seem to matter to her tonight.

Her emotions were so raw, so close to the surface that without a distraction, she feared she'd be overtaken by them as soon as Jeremy was gone. "I would like to ask you to stay with me a little longer."

"Stay? Here in your room?"

She shrugged. "I don't want to be alone with my thoughts tonight."

Jeremy rubbed her arms briskly. "I can stay for a while if you have need of me."

"I do."

He walked to the window and parted the drapes until enough moonlight spilled across the chamber to make everything clearer. He returned and his fingers immediately rose to her hair, then he was removing the pins. "Let's get you more comfortable then."

His fingers were nimble as he removed and discarded the jewels she had worn about her neck, too, placing them across her dressing table. He turned her about and began to unbutton her gown —more quickly than a man bent on seduction, and as efficient as any maid Fanny had ever employed. He urged her to sit on the edge of her bed, and he fell to his knees to remove her slippers. Then he untied the garters holding up her silk stockings, which he rolled down her legs.

Fanny experienced a moment of misgiving

then. She hardly knew this man, and she was allowing him to ready her for bed.

She put her hand over her chest, holding up her gown so it didn't fall and expose her breasts.

Jeremy drew back. "Where is your nightgown, my lady?"

She gulped. "Behind the dressing screen."

He looked there and then at her again, and nodded. "If you need help to manage the rest on your own just call out."

Fanny rushed for the privacy of the dressing screen and, once hidden from his view, put her hands over her flaming cheeks. She peeked over the top of the screen, only to find Jeremy turning back her bedding and then sitting on the edge of the mattress to wait for her return. Fanny squirmed out of her loosened gown, removed her stays and chemise and then rushed to pull her nightgown over her head. She considered donning a robe, but she wanted to make it clear she was bound for sleep and nothing else.

Feeling shy, she emerged from her corner and Jeremy was immediately on his feet. He held out his hand and guided her to bed as if she were a young child and not a grown woman older than him. He covered her with the bedding, snuggling the material around her shoulders, before closing the drapes almost completely. Just a tiny sliver of light illuminated him, and she thought she saw a smile curve his lips. He came closer to the bed and brushed her long hair back from her face with a gentleness she'd not felt for so long. Not since her husband had lived had anyone worried about her in such a way.

She caught his hand in hers and squeezed his fingers tight. "Thank you for tonight."

"My pleasure. All of it," he said, and started to pull away.

But Fanny could not seem to let him go.

He looked back at her, surprised. "Lady Rivers?"

She wet her lips. "Would you…could you remain a little longer?"

"For how long?"

"Until dawn."

He drew in a deep breath. "If you need me, I'll stay."

Relief coursed through her that she wouldn't be alone, and she finally released his fingers.

Jeremy glided around the bed quietly, removing his coat and his pocket watch to place them on a side table. She felt a pang of disquiet as he removed his boots that he might continue undressing until he was naked. But then he climbed onto the bed mostly clothed and wriggled closer, spreading one arm out toward her.

"Come here, my dear lady. Hold on to me."

Fanny rolled into his embrace and heaved a heavy sigh as he wrapped her in his arms.

"Today must have been dreadful for you. I'm so sorry," he whispered.

"I am, too. I don't even know who I'm grieving

for, and I feel quite bad about that." A sob tore from her throat, though she tried to smother it.

Jeremy's fingers stroked her head and hair. "It's all right. I'm here."

Fanny breathed his scent deep into her lungs, conscious that the beat of his heart was steady and true had pushed away the impulse to cry. Jeremy was young, healthy. Certain to live for a very long time. And with that thought in her mind, Fanny felt peace for the first time in hours.

Chapter Six

Jeremy accepted a silver tankard from a servant and strolled into the Duke of Stapleton's library, overcome by the unexpected noise of masculinity but determined not to show he didn't belong in such a room. The vast chamber contained at least two dozen other men of varying ages, each wearing a band of mourning around their upper left arm. One of the servants had whispered to him that most, if not all of the local gentry had answered the duke's summons to toast the late Mr. Hawthorne today.

Knowing few in the room but asked to attend as well, Jeremy kept to the outskirts of the conversations and observed everyone. A great deal they spoke of meant nothing to him, but he prowled the room as if he was used to such gatherings.

It was clear to see who possessed the most wealth or the least by the way they held themselves and the tones of their voices. Signet rings sparkled on chubby fingers and fob watches gleamed in waistcoat pockets of the richest fellows. More than a few boasted canes topped with gold figures of lions or horses, all but a few spoke with subdued tones.

He passed a pair of toffs with heads bent together speaking loudly. "I say, where are the women?"

"I heard they've all gone to comfort the new widow for the day," the sadder of the pair muttered and then buried his nose in his tankard.

"A shame for I had wished to speak with one of them alone."

The sadder man glanced sideways at his companion. "Still hoping to catch Lady Rivers? Good luck to you."

"Always. You haven't given up, I'm sure of that."

"I have my own reasons for seeking her out." The sadder one sighed. "She's led us all a merry dance over the years."

"For the last year, I promise you," claimed Lord Dour, as Jeremy dubbed him. "One way or the other, she'll be wed before the year is out."

"Ambitious." The balding one asked, "Keen to expand the family holdings?"

The sour fellow was narrowly built and at least twenty years older than Jeremy. His face displayed little sorrow as he regarded the occupants of the room. "Always, and now with Hawthorne soon to be underground, the widow will finally have to sell her slice of land. What a better time to unite two great families. Women have no business managing an estate or money."

The balding one sighed. "And Lady Rivers has a surfeit of both just waiting to be taken over."

"I can certainly imagine better uses for it than building orphanages and the like," Lord Dour nearly spat as if it was a dirty habit to help someone in need. "Well, let's drink to Hawthorne and hope the ladies return before sunset."

Jeremy moved away but committed those men and their words to his memory, though not with the intention of emulating them on the stage one day. He did not like the way they spoke of Lady Rivers. *One way or another* meant she really was a target for fortune hunters at this wedding.

He had wondered if she'd been exaggerating in the beginning, but now…

Apparently not.

And after last night, giving her the comfort she craved in her own bed, he was even more determined to look out for her best interests.

The bald fellow raised his glass high. "To Hawthorne."

Jeremy toasted along with them before he strolled on. But he decided to find out who they were and then…well, he had options if they caused trouble for Lady Rivers later. He could at least warn her, or perhaps the duke might want to know as well. He seemed quite a protective father.

Eventually he found the duke seated by the fire with all the male members of his family surrounding him. Jeremy eased a little closer and was grateful when he was called over by the duke himself to join them.

"I was wondering what was keeping you."

"There's quite a crowd," he murmured by way of apology.

"Indeed there is, and rightly so. It's a damn shame about Hawthorne," the Duke of Stapleton said, taking a long swallow from the silver tankard a footman had placed before him.

The man's sons, son-in-law and future son-in-law murmured their agreement and drank deeply. Jeremy merely sipped his ale to be agreeable, not out of any real desire for the drink.

The death of the neighbor seemed to have hit the family hard, the duke most of all. There had even been talk of delaying the wedding out of respect for the dead, but the newly widowed Mrs. Hawthorne had foreseen such a decision. She had sent a note forbidding anyone to consider delaying the nuptials. So the wedding would take place a few days earlier than planned, with the funeral to follow a day later.

He had to admit it was hard to look forward to a wedding when the dead was waiting for burial not far away.

After the wedding, he'd been told the Westfalls would observe three months of mourning for their dear departed friend and neighbor. Everyone from duke down to pot boy would clad themselves in black and the house would close to guests. He'd already seen signs of preparations being made by servants on his way down. He wasn't sure what would happen to his visit to the country, but he assumed Lady Rivers would eventually send him back to London before his two weeks were up.

He sipped his ale and contemplated his own demise. Would anyone even notice he was gone? Would he be famous by then and mourned by hundreds of ardent admirers? Would he be mourned the way Mr. Hawthorne was? By a woman who couldn't imagine life without him?

Life carried on unscripted and adlibbed. It was only in a play that an actor could ever know the fate of the character he played.

He buried his nose in his tankard. Mr. Hawthorne's passing had made him maudlin and the drink certainly wasn't helping. Jeremy had never been much for overindulgence of spirits or ale, but the Westfalls appeared to be seasoned campaigners of such indulgences. He was trying to fit in by appearing to share their vices. He took note of Lord Rafferty reaching for a new tankard and took a hasty pretend sip of his, so no one would offer to fetch him more.

The gathering of men eventually split into small groups, each one taking turns to venture close to the duke for a few words before drifting away again. But soon the talk was not of the dearly departed but of the future.

The duke sighed heavily after one group departed. "Of course, the daughter's chances of making a match now are in tatters for another year. Can't accept suitors calling on her now until their mourning is over."

"They'll mourn the full two years," Mr. Whitfield explained to Jeremy.

"A pair of women, one widowed, one unwed, with only young children to lend a hand will struggle," Rafferty warned. "Rebecca is concerned how they'll fare in the years to come."

"I expect the estate might need to be sold," Whitfield said quietly.

"No. Mrs. Hawthorne will have help, whether she agrees to it or not," the duke vowed. "I owe it to Hawthorne to look out for them. He was the best of men. I'll buy the farm if need be to keep them with a roof over their heads. Gillian wants to take the eldest to London with us when she's out of mourning and give her a chance to make a good match there."

"It is good of her to take such an interest," Jeremy murmured, feeling he should add something to the conversation. "A match will surely be made with the duchess' help."

They all nodded, staring into their tankards before drinking deeply again.

Jeremy was starting to feel the effects of the drink he'd consumed and set his tankard aside. He had to keep his wits about him, to stay in character for the whole two weeks. Thankfully, no one seemed inclined to do more than drink for now.

The duke and those gathered closest appeared to be firm friends all. Rafferty, soon to be married into the family, was freely helping himself to a fresh tankard without leave, Whitfield swiped the duke's tankard from his hand and refilled it without saying a word.

Whitfield did not drink as much as the others, Jeremy noted, but his sadness was palpable. "Jessica has decided to stay another night with the Hawthornes. Natalia needs help with the little ones."

"That leaves the widow and the farm to be managed."

Jeremy knew little about the managing of a farm other than what he'd overheard last night. "Lady Rivers mentioned the land seemed to be in decline."

All eyes turned on him.

The duke smashed his fist on the arm of his chair suddenly. "I should have seen it. But of course, Fanny has always been a sharp one. It pains me that I didn't realize until now that they were struggling. I could have been of help earlier, and perhaps…"

Perhaps Hawthorne would have lived longer? Jeremy shook his head and stood, snatching up his tankard. His tongue suddenly could not stay silent. "Death comes to all on silent wings to cease suffering but often brings regret to those left behind in its wake. It is the way of the world, and naught can be done to stand in death's path. We must stand together and face the challenges of the here and now as men of compassion and hope."

Everyone stared at him.

"The soul of a poet," Whitfield observed with a slight smile.

The duke sighed heavily. "Truer words have never been spoken, though. Hawthorne's pain has ended and ours just begun, I fear."

The man who'd been hoping to catch Lady Rivers approached and offered his condolences. "Sad times, your grace," he murmured. "Sad times indeed."

The duke stood to shake his hand. "Thank you for coming, Lord Thwaite. I'll be sure to tell Hawthorne's widow you mourned with us today when I see her next."

Thwaite nodded. "No need. I shall pay my respects to her soon myself."

"That is kind of you," the duke murmured, quickly losing interest.

Kind? The man was planning to buy the lady's property for a song and probably throw them out into the cold before the year was over.

The balding man joined them next, dropping into Jeremy's recently vacated chair. "Any idea when the ladies might return?"

"Not soon," the duke announced.

Jeremy was watching Lord Thwaite's face and saw a flicker of anger at the news. He very quickly excused himself and slipped from the chamber. Jeremy was happy that he had gone, but hoped he wasn't headed straight for the Hawthorne property to pressure the widow to sell to him.

He turned his attention to the balding fellow

who had remained. So far, no one had said his name out loud.

Lord Samuel moved to stand beside Jeremy. "That's Letterford, he owns the Heybridge estate about three miles south of here."

"Thank you. No one has thought to introduce us yet."

"No one ever does. He's an amiable old fellow. Widowed. His children are grown. The man who just left was Lord Thwaite. His heir is expected to arrive in time for the wedding, I hear. He's to stand up with Rafferty as best man."

"Where is Thwaite's property located?"

"A little closer. You could say his property is nearly a neighbor to my father's estate."

A few things he'd heard clicked into place inside his head. "Is it because of the Hawthorne land's location, that it's not?"

"Yes, that's right. I'm surprised that you would realize that."

Jeremy shrugged. "I must have overheard something about it earlier, I suppose."

Lord Samuel was quiet for a moment and then he whispered, "What exactly did you hear?"

Jeremy glanced at the duke's second son, the scoundrel spare, and shrugged. "Thwaite mentioned a plan for expansion."

"Not with the Hawthornes' land?"

Jeremy held his stare. "It's what he hinted at."

Lord Samuel scowled fiercely. "Couldn't wait

till the old fellow was buried before making a move on the widow."

"I don't think he's done anything yet," Jeremy admitted. "He mentioned a lack of funds."

"Thwaite has been eyeing that property for years. Excuse me. I think I should call on the new widow. My children have no doubt ventured there again."

Lord Samuel whispered in his father's ear and then strode off out of the room.

The duke frowned after him, but then shrugged. "Do you know Hawthorne could always best me with a bow? Devilishly clever shot with it. Mind you, he couldn't shoot down game with anything else. Remember that time we all went out and he shot off the tip of the tallest tree on my land?"

"We were just boys then," murmured Lord Milo, the duke's heir.

"You and I tried to be just like him that summer," Whitfield added with a smile.

Lord Milo frowned. "Didn't Hawthorne keep that bit of tree as a souvenir?"

The duke nodded. "Yes, it's in his study to this day. We always have a good laugh whenever I visit him." The duke's lips pressed together firmly. "When I *had*..."

Whitfield clapped the duke on his shoulder when it appeared Stapleton had become too emotional to continue speaking. That had happened a few times in the past day. Whitfield raised a glass high. "To our friend and his poor aim with a rifle."

"To Hawthorne."

Glasses were raised, drunk from, and then silence, the gentlemen each falling into their own introspections. Lord Milo left to circulate with the remaining guests until they departed.

When Lord Letterford finally took his leave, Whitfield raised his head and stared at Jeremy. "This must have put a damper on your visit to the countryside."

"Not at all. I mean to say that if I am any kind of gentleman, I should support my lady's family in good times and in bad."

The duke turned to Whitfield. "He speaks well, doesn't he?"

"Indeed."

Rafferty cleared his throat. "Has Letterford spoken to you yet?"

"No."

"He will." Rafferty cast a look in Jeremy's direction. "It concerns Fanny."

The duke's eyes flicked to Jeremy before he said, "Fanny is a grown woman. I have no say in how she lives her life. She's already turned Letterford down once. He'd be a fool to ask again."

Rafferty's expression soured. "I thought time might have changed her mind."

"It won't be time that changes her mind, and you should know that as well as anyone here."

Rafferty frowned. "Do you still have a man in her household?"

Jeremy gaped as the duke nodded and confirm that he did in fact spy on his eldest daughter. "He lets me know of any potential problems."

Given the way the duke's attention returned to Jeremy, it was clear he considered Jeremy a potential problem. He had met a number of the household staff already and hadn't detected anything untoward about any of them. "Who is your spy?"

"Why?"

"Merely curious how one might act such a role and avoid detection," he promised with a shrug. "I've little chance of meeting a real spy who would admit to it."

The duke smiled tightly. "I could tell you so you could learn from them, but can I count on you not to tell my daughter, Mr. Dawes?"

Jeremy owed his loyalty to Fanny, not to her father the duke. He shook his head.

The duke sighed. "Well, at least she found herself an uncorruptible one this time. The last fellow she plucked from obscurity could be bribed to do anything for anyone."

Jeremy scowled. "I'm sorry to hear it."

"Never fear, I will always deal with anyone who acts against my daughter's best interests," the duke promised.

Jeremy nodded, understanding that the responsibility of his current role shouldn't be taken lightly or he'd suffer for any presumption. The duke would *deal with him* too if Jeremy strayed beyond his current role.

He'd no intention of doing so. But he walked a fine line where propriety was concerned. He had to make it seem like he was in serious pursuit of Lady Rivers without jeopardizing her reputation.

The duke rearranged his long limbs and regarded his tankard yet again. "I hope you are as loyal to my daughter as you seem, Mr. Dawes. If not, you will not fare well." The duke's jaw clenched, determination clear on his features.

"Understood." Jeremy nodded, feeling a pang of uneasiness. He'd been threatened before by rough men all his life. Men holding knives, blunderbusses pointed at him. Men who would murder and never be held to account. But he had to admit, being threatened by the well-dressed head of the Westfall family was actually equally terrifying. The duke had the power to send him back to his old life, deny him his profession, or even make him disappear altogether.

"Good." The duke nodded and then abruptly turned to his elder son who'd just returned. "How long will you be staying at Stapleton this time, son?"

Talk resumed without Jeremy, and soon the duke appeared to forget his presence as servants appeared, lighting dozens of candles about the chamber.

When Fanny had suggested he take on this

role, she'd failed to mention her family was so protective. He didn't mind that they were, but he wasn't a threat to her freedom. He was definitely in uncharted waters here, but he'd made promises to Fanny he intended to keep. He meant to be a man of his word, but he was beginning to suspect that no one in this place would ever believe him.

The ladies returned finally, subdued and their spirits low. Along with the duke and the other gentlemen, Jeremy made his way out to meet their carriage. The duchess seemed larger than ever and walked slowly toward her husband. Lord Milo went to her other side and helped get her up the stairs and inside. Jeremy waited for Fanny, finding her the last to exit the carriage.

He smiled to see her and held out his hand to steady her descent. "How are you this evening?"

"Glad to see you," she promised. She paused and then looked up at him. "I had hoped you'd be here. Where is everyone?"

"I believe most wedding guests have gone to find their own amusements," he promised. They took two steps toward the manor before Jeremy was forced to revise his statement.

Thwaite hadn't departed after all and nor had Lord Samuel.

"Good evening, sister," Lord Samuel murmured as he hurried to kiss her cheek, but whispered something Jeremy couldn't quite catch in her ear too. He drew back. "How was Clarice when you left her? Already retired for the night, I hope."

"She's utterly exhausted. Jessica has remained behind and has asked for Whitfield to join her there tonight." Fanny nodded to Lord Thwaite. "My lord."

"Sad times," he replied. "Sad times indeed to lose such a dear friend."

Thwaite bestowed a patently false sadness on his face that wouldn't fool any audience in any theater. "He was much admired."

"I must change for dinner," Fanny murmured to Jeremy.

Jeremy, aware they had an audience watching with his own agenda, brought Fanny's hand to his lips and faked a kiss upon her glove. "I'll be here."

After a moment's consideration, she inclined her head. "Until then."

"I can hardly wait," Jeremy promised. He escorted her to the base of the stairs, and affected a smitten sigh when she was out of sight. And then, with Thwaite watching him still, he sauntered back into the library as if he belonged there.

Chapter Seven

Fanny's face ached with the strain of forcing herself to smile for the guests who prowled the halls and drawing room at Stapleton Manor later that same night. The festivities for Rebecca and Lord Rafferty's wedding had been cancelled out of respect for the dead but no one seemed inclined to not gather together.

Fanny slipped from the drawing room, into the dark and empty ballroom, aware by the time she'd made the halfway point that footsteps followed. It was probably Jeremy Dawes. He'd been her shadow for most of the night. And it had been nice to have him close at hand when Thwaite was so clearly in pursuit. She'd be worried about him if he didn't already have a wife tucked away at home forgotten and neglected.

But she had other reasons to be grateful for Jeremy's presence. He'd been instrumental in changing the subject a number of times when the discussion of death had upset her.

Of course, he hadn't only been with her. He had circulated the room, speaking with her father and brothers, who were brooding, and becoming known to friends and neighbors as well.

He'd even run an errand for Rebecca, which

had put a smile on Rebecca's face for at least half a minute. They had talked together, but of nothing of any real consequence.

Perhaps because of her sadness, he had not brought up the fact she'd slept in his arms last night. And for that she was grateful, because she didn't quite know what had come over her even now. Her emotions felt too raw when she considered yesterday and last night. She'd been weak to show her emotions to a man who barely knew her, and that wasn't like her.

When she stepped outside onto the terrace, she pulled in a lungful of the cooler county air and let it out slowly, hoping to feel more like herself soon.

The Stapleton grounds were awash with moonlight and appeared magical. She could almost imagine she was alone.

Jeremy stopped beside her. "It's quiet out here."

She was aware of his eyes upon her but kept hers on the view. "Hmm."

"I hope you don't mind that I followed you. I was concerned." He shook out a shawl, which Fanny must have left behind on a forgotten chair some time ago."

She allowed him to drape it across her shoulders and pulled it tight around her chest for comfort. "There's no reason for concern. I just needed a moment to myself."

"I'll leave you be then."

She glanced up at him, startled by how much

she didn't want that. "It wasn't you driving me away from everyone tonight."

"I'm glad." Jeremy dug his finger under his neckcloth and tugged. Fanny had noticed him doing that earlier at dinner, several times actually.

She turned fully to face him. "You look uncomfortable, sir. Let me see if I can help loosen that for you."

He lifted his chin. "I should have gone up and fixed it, but I didn't want to leave you at the mercy of your admirers."

"They are persistent, even today."

"Shoddy way to treat you. Following you from one side of the room to the other. It's clear you're not yourself."

"That's what they were counting on." He held still as Fanny tried to loosen the knot just a little bit more. "This knot has not been your usual style," she noted.

"The duke suggested I try something more formal for the evening," he murmured. "I like the way it looks but not how it hugs so damn tight about my throat."

She worked on the knot carefully, trying her best not to ruin it. "In my experience, gentlemen usually favor just one or two styles of knot for their cravat." She frowned. "Why have you started taking advice from my father on how to dress?"

"It's a habit from the theater. We actors always consult each other when dressing for a new role."

He laughed. "It also seems a good way to stay on the duke's good side."

"Father only has good sides. He's the easiest of men."

Jeremy snorted as if he didn't believe her, but she ignored the chance to set him straight while she finished her adjustment. Jeremy could learn a lot from her father, but perhaps not about cravats. "There, done."

He rubbed his throat. "Ah, that is so much better. Thank you, my lady."

He beamed at her—and Fanny's heart gave the most alarming lurch in response. As she stared up into his handsome face, a feeling of disquiet filled her. Jeremy was an actor playing the role of her admirer. She would do well not to mistake his interest for something real.

Fanny turned away and looked up. "I've always loved this time of year at Stapleton. The skies are so clear at night. As a child, I always thought I should be able to reach up and touch the stars, they're so close."

"I can easily believe you," Jeremy murmured, looking up, too. He stretched up his hand, fingers reaching for the bright points of light above them. "You don't get this sort of view when you grow up in the gutter."

She turned to Jeremy. "Tell me about that."

"I'd rather not." Jeremy stubbornly shook his head. "The future is all that matters, or so a very learned woman told me the day she took me on."

She blushed. "A happy day that was for me."

"I'm not sure your family would agree with that now. Don't take this the wrong way, but your father and brothers gathered together are almost as frightening as my childhood was."

"They mean you no harm."

He snorted.

"Papa already knows how we met. I told him this, my little play, was my idea and not yours."

Jeremy shook his head. "He must have been shocked."

Fanny shrugged, trying not to remember the expression that had graced her father's face when she'd told him she'd hired an actor to play the part of her lover. But she'd explained and reassured him it was only make-believe. "I'm a grown woman and my business is my own. He can do nothing."

Jeremy crossed his arms over his chest. "I'm sure he knows how to make a man who crosses him disappear."

Fanny laughed. The idea of her father seriously threatening anyone, let alone Jeremy Dawes, was ludicrous. "My gut, as you men call it, told me that you were a sound investment."

Jeremy sighed. "Women's intuition is flawed."

She was taken aback by his statement. Never before had she heard him speak dismissively of women, or her, in her presence before. "I don't think—"

He drew closer and lowered his voice, "Now, don't misunderstand what I'm saying. You are a brilliant woman. Astute at business as any man, I hear, but when it comes to people, it's not your head making decisions for you, but your heart. You ought to be more cautious who you trust with your confidences."

"You are worried that someone might learn about last night?"

He nodded.

"Nothing happened between us. Not even a kiss."

He drew closer still, his voice a low rumble as he continued, "No one would believe I wouldn't have tried for that or more. You were upset, vulnerable."

She had been; she still was around him. She swallowed and squared her shoulders. "We know the truth. Nothing happened."

"Any man would be a fool not to try to win your favor. There are plenty of men…lords… trying to catch your eye even tonight. Why would you not let one of them catch you?"

Fanny crossed her arms over her chest, and it stopped Jeremy's encroachment. "You've been listening to Papa and my brothers say I should marry," she accused.

"I cannot avoid them or hearing things of that nature." Jeremy nodded. "Your father mentioned others had taken advantage of you in the past and is suspicious of me too. He warned me not to be another, or I'd regret it, and I swear I will not stray beyond the terms of our contract. But I can easily see how to go about it. Bemoan a lack of funds and your reticule flies open. You believe all people are essentially good."

"Everyone has good in them," she protested.

"And so many choose to do ill instead," he said with a scowl. "People say they care about others all the time and mean it less than a quarter. People are never completely honest."

Fanny stared at him in surprise. Was he warning her to distrust him, too?

There was so much about Jeremy that she did not know, and so much he wouldn't say. His past was as murky as the Thames, and he didn't like to talk about his future beyond the next play. But he had to make plans. He could not hope to stumble from one performance to another and expect to succeed brilliantly. "I think your past experiences have clouded your judgement. I think—"

"Ah, there you are, Lady Rivers!" Lord Thwaite exclaimed jovially as he joined them in the moonlight. "And you are by her side again, Mr. Dawes. I'm surprised you're not off making yourself known to the young ladies and charming them."

"It's hardly the time to charm anyone," Jeremy noted, in a voice so devoid of warmth that she almost shivered in dread.

Fanny hadn't heard anyone approaching across the ballroom's hardwood floor, and she really should have. How much of their conversation had Thwaite heard before interrupting? "Mr. Dawes was just telling me about his hope for a fascinating new play," Fanny told Thwaite, stepping between them. "I so look forward to seeing him perform again."

Thwaite smirked and then wiped the expression clean. "Perhaps we'll watch him together in the future. The view from my box is exceptional."

"She already has a box," Jeremy said flatly, moving to her side. "The best box in the theater is right by the stage, and she owns it."

"Yes, I have always had a great interest in the theater," she enthused. "I never miss a performance when in London, especially not when Jeremy is onstage."

Thwaite's eyes darted to Jeremy and, in the darkness, she sensed they narrowed in suspicion. "Well, now I must discover for myself what sort of *performer* he really is."

Fanny felt the hair on the back of her neck rise in warning, but she dismissed the sensation. She had wanted people to believe Jeremy was a romantic interest of hers and leave her to it. From Thwaite, she sensed a keen interest to discover the whole truth. Time to distract *him*. "And now, having availed myself of the view and the tranquil country air, I was just about to return inside to encourage my sister to play."

"It would be a pleasure to escort you," Thwaite said quickly, depriving Jeremy of the chance.

She reluctantly placed her hand Thwaite's

sleeve. "Mr. Dawes was just remarking upon the difference in the clarity of the stars when in the country compared to the lack in London."

Thwaite looked down at her. "'Tis a prettier view at Stapleton indeed." Fanny caught a flicker of smug satisfaction on Thwaite's face before he turned her away from Jeremy. "Do excuse us, sir."

"Certainly. But I will be returning to the drawing room, as well."

Thwaite leaned his head closer to hers. "Have you given any thought to the Hampton Street project?"

"Not as yet."

"It will be a very profitable enterprise," he enthused. "I have every confidence we can overcome current difficulties with an injection of new money from discerning investors like yourself."

"That, I shall decide for myself at a later time."

"We should meet to discuss the project. I wouldn't want anyone catching wind of our partnership too soon and having you lose your chance to join your friends."

She shrugged. Fanny was a little too tired for business talk tonight. "I shall look into the matter when I have a spare moment, my lord."

Thwaite had the sense not to press her and took her toward the fire, where her father sat on a long chaise and guided her down to sit beside him.

Jeremy stopped not far away and caught her eye. "Would you care for a refreshment, my lady?"

She smiled at Jeremy and he smiled back, while her silly heart gave another ridiculous jump in her chest. "A sherry would be lovely, Mr. Dawes. Thank you."

"Your grace?"

Father held up his empty glass. He was taking Hawthorne's death very hard. Drinking more than could be good for him. "A refill, port, please."

"My pleasure," Jeremy murmured before turning toward the array of decanters lined up across the room.

Lord Thwaite squeezed in beside her as Lord Letterford dropped into a chair that faced her and Father. Fanny had an uncomfortable feeling that, if not for Father's presence, she'd just been surrounded.

After Jeremy returned with a drink for her and her father, he remained nearby, keeping a watchful eye over her again. She was rather glad she'd not had to ask him to do that.

"There's been a lot of talk about your Cedar Mill of late," Thwaite mused.

Fanny sipped her drink before she answered. Her investment in Cedar Mill was no secret...but the changes she'd planned to make were supposed to be still. "Such as?"

"Is it true you're in negotiations to sell it to that upstart Maxwell Danvers, of all people?"

Fanny worked hard to keep the surprise from her face. Her discussions with Danvers were in the very early stages. "The mill belongs to me."

"You'd be a fool to sell to him at any price," Thwaite warned.

Men were always ready to tell her what she should or should not do as if she had no intelligence. The state of her fortune proved she knew exactly what she was doing without any man's interference. She turned her head to regard Thwaite with not a little hostility. "You are entitled to your opinion, I suppose."

"Yes, and—"

Father put up his hand. "No business discussions tonight."

Lord Thwaite appeared ready to protest but finally subsided. "We'll continue our discussion another time. To Hawthorne."

Glasses were raised around the room and Fanny sipped her sherry slowly.

Father sighed, staring into his glass. "I don't feel like this, after all. Dawes, be a good fellow and take this from me. I'm suddenly in the mood to play a bit of music instead of drowning myself in drink. You may take my place here if you like," Father murmured.

Fanny was relieved when Jeremy crossed the room to take the glass from her father. He slid into the vacated seat beside Fanny's and a great deal of her annoyance with Thwaite slipped away.

Father started up on the pianoforte, a familiar tune she knew well, and she lost herself in the music and happy memories of times past. Father had done just the thing to lift her spirits.

She turned to Jeremy, who was sitting somewhat stiffly on the edge of the chair beside her. "I was hoping my father would play during your visit. He is very skilled on the pianoforte. Some of my favorite memories are of falling asleep here with my sisters while he entertained us in the evenings."

Jeremy's body softened in her direction a touch. "Did your late mother play, as well?"

"Mama had no talent for music, but the current Lady Stapleton does and plays beautifully," she murmured. "At long last, Father now has someone to play duets with."

"I look forward to having the opportunity of hearing them play together then," Jeremy whispered, and then sat back like she had to listen, his fingers tapping on one bent knee.

Lord Thwaite leaned close to whisper in her ear, startling her. "Now your father is occupied, we can talk about that Mill uninterrupted."

Father came to an abrupt halt. "Fanny, be a dear and come and turn the pages for your old father."

"You're not old, Papa," Fanny exclaimed, jumping to her feet immediately and rushing to do his bidding to get away from Thwaite. His breath across her ear had not been a pleasant sensation. Not like Jeremy's had been last night when he'd held her.

Father didn't actually need sheet music when he played, but she was willing to go along with his request. He gave her a long considering look as he made room for her and started up again.

Fanny dutifully pretended to turn page after page. It wasn't long before Lord Thwaite got up and called out good night to everyone before stalking off for his chambers upstairs. She hadn't been aware he'd be staying tonight and hoped not to see him over breakfast tomorrow morning. Letterford and a few others went with him, thankfully, leaving only her family members and Jeremy behind.

Jeremy had leaned back in his chair and closed his eyes to listen to her father play. She studied his handsome face in repose…and something inside her softened. She admired him openly; how could she not? But it had never been his face that had drawn her notice. It was the way he flirted, the way he never sought her favor or coin. It was the way he laughed at everything she took for granted.

"You remind me of your mother tonight," father said, drawing her attention back to him.

"I do?" Fanny had never thought she resembled her mother very much, who'd been beautiful but flighty and vain and contrary. Possessed of fierce intelligence and stunning selfishness sometimes, too. It was a sad truth that Fanny's life had become less unpredictable after she was gone. "Why tonight?"

"Your mother was forever being pestered by ambitious men."

Fanny leaned lightly against her father's

shoulder. "Mother would never have betrayed you, or the family interests."

"Oh, I know that," he promised. "But some men seem to think persistence will be rewarded anyway and they keep returning, like a bad smell."

She hoped that would not be the case with Thwaite. "I'm still not convinced I should invest in Thwaite's new venture."

"It's not his venture or sudden interest in Cedar Mill that worries me," Father murmured. "It's him. He's got his eye on you for something, sweetheart."

Fanny straightened up.

"Oh, I'm sure you've the sense to feel it already, which is why Dawes is following you about so closely tonight. Thwaite had quite a sour look about him when you both slipped away together earlier."

"I've never encouraged him to imagine I would be interested in him that way. Besides, he's married."

"Married men betray their wives, and some men don't bother to wait for an invitation either." Father frowned momentarily as he played a difficult passage. "Do you know the story of how Thwaite acquired his country estate?"

"It was part of his first wife's dowry, wasn't it?"

Father nodded. "Thwaite ruined her to force the match."

Fanny's blood ran cold. "He wouldn't dare force me."

"No, perhaps not under my roof, but I'd prefer you not face that same situation somewhere else. Oh, I know you're a woman of experience now, and widows often do as they please. But he could create enough of a fuss to damage your reputation beyond repair. He'd make it seem that your only choice was to give him what he wants. Be careful. He pressed me hard to stay the night. I won't have you unhappy. Keep Dawes close."

Fanny blinked as Father suddenly cut his performance short and stood to address the room. "Milo, Samuel. I've just remembered a matter that requires a discussion between us."

Father popped a kiss on her head and went off toward his study with her startled brothers, leaving Fanny and Jeremy as the only two souls left in the room.

Jeremy regarded her drowsily. "What did I miss?"

She chuckled. "Nothing of importance. You should go to bed."

"Not until you retire." He climbed to his feet and stretched his long agile limbs. "Do you play the pianoforte as well?"

"Do you think musical talent runs in every great family?" Fanny banged her fingers down on the keys, inelegantly as always.

"Stop, stop," Jeremy cried, putting his hands over his ears. "I would have accepted *no* without any proof. At least now I'm fully awake."

Fanny smiled, running her fingers along the

keys, the most pleasing sound she'd ever made on the instrument, before covering them up. "It's not a talent I've ever aspired to possess."

"His grace plays very well. Better than anything I've ever heard. Almost put me to sleep."

"Almost? I'm fairly sure I heard a snore." Fanny put the music sheets away in their usual place.

"I do not snore," he insisted. "And I was only resting my eyelids until you had need of me."

When she turned around to respond, Jeremy was peeking out the windows.

He grinned. "Stars are still out."

She laughed. "Did you expect them to disappear so quickly?"

"They do in London."

She strolled toward him, drawn to his smile and the warmth she remembered finding in his arms. "You are not in London anymore, my dear sir. You are in the country, where the skies are often clear for hours on end and the soot and fog rarely inconvenience anyone for long. The weather wouldn't dare be anything but perfect for my sister's wedding day. Father wouldn't allow it."

Jeremy laughed. "You know, your father has your sense of humor."

"I think it's the other way round, sir." Fanny took after her father far more than she might have her mother and was proud of that. She suddenly yawned, though she tried to hide it. She didn't want to be alone yet, but parting from Jeremy was a certainty.

Jeremy presented his arm. "Might I offer my paltry escort upstairs, my lady?"

"Indeed, you may. It has been a very long day indeed."

Fanny slipped her arm through Jeremy's and felt...*safe*. Content. The discomfort of being pursued by Lord Thwaite slipped away slowly.

"What was your father whispering to you?"

She didn't have to tell Jeremy about Father's warning, but she wanted to. "He warned that Lord Thwaite has an interest in me."

"He does."

Fanny blinked. "How did you deduce that?"

"He said as much to Lord Letterford when the men gathered to mourn Mr. Hawthorne earlier today." Jeremy looked down on her with a frown. "I wager that's why he wrangled an invitation to stay the night. Letterford, too, has an interest in you, but he's not as obvious about it."

"I certainly do not have an interest in any of the guests staying at Stapleton."

Jeremy pulled an excessively sad face. "I'm sorry to hear I'm boring you."

"I meant guests other than you," she promised. That feeling of being flustered crept back. "Oh, this is dreadful. Thwaite and Letterford, I mean."

"You are the last Westfall daughter in want of a husband. I'm sure there are wagers written in any number of betting books."

"I don't need a husband. I have you," she promised.

"For two weeks, and then it's back to the theater for me," Jeremy reminded her.

"I think I'll miss having you around all the time," she whispered.

"We will see each other at the theater," he promised, "and perhaps you'll want my escort to other places, too."

Yes she could but suddenly that didn't feel like enough anymore.

Chapter Eight

"Thank you for a wonderful evening, my lady," Jeremy murmured as Lady Rivers' hand fell from his sleeve at the top of the stairs. Her room was one way, his the other.

She hesitated but then smiled. "Good night, sir. Sleep well."

"You, too."

He watched her go, feeling rather glad he had come to the country. Protecting Fanny from fortune hunters and cheering her up wasn't all that hard to do and left him with a good feeling around his heart.

She was almost at her door when she suddenly drew back from it.

"Jeremy!" she called, gesturing to him with one hand to join her urgently.

The tone of her voice caused the hair to rise all over his body. Jeremy rushed to her side.

Fanny had her hand at her throat as she whispered, "My door is open."

"Perhaps a maid left it that way?"

"No. It was locked when I went down to dinner, and no one should have reason to enter without informing me."

Jeremy leaned past Fanny and nudged the door open wider with his foot. He peered into the dark recesses of the chamber and saw nothing and no one to cause alarm immediately. But he stepped around Fanny and entered the darkened bedchamber ahead of her. He crossed the room to the windows and flung open the drapes—hoping not to reveal an intruder by moonlight.

As far as he could see, the chamber *was* empty now.

But it was not as neat as he expected it to be. Not like last night, when they'd returned to Stapleton late after the long day of grief.

He went to the hearth and stirred the fire to life. When he had a flame, he lit a few candles around the room and turned to study the chamber.

There were books spread out across Fanny's bed, open, as if someone had been flicking through them. Someone had clearly been in her room while she had been downstairs. He grew very angry when he spied drawers open and undergarments haphazardly hanging from them. No thief would ever leave so obvious a sign of their actions. It invited an investigation.

"Someone has indeed been here, Fanny, but they are long gone," he announced, beckoning her to come and look for herself.

Fanny rushed into the room and spun around wildly, horror written all over her face. "My books and journals are out. My jewels?" She raced around the chamber, checking into all the nooks and crannies where she must have stored her possessions. She sagged. "Nothing has been taken. Thank God."

Jeremy knew all about stealing. How not to leave a trace that you'd ransacked a chamber. Whoever had done this was an amateur and in a hurry, or had another motive. "Are you sure nothing was stolen?"

She combed through her jewel box a second time. "Yes. Who could possibly have done this?"

Jeremy quietly pushed the door shut. The houseguests sprang to mind, but they were all peers and he couldn't accuse one without proof. "Are you sure everything is accounted for?"

"I believe so. But the information in my journals…" Her eyes narrowed. "That is not for public consumption."

He passed a journal to her. "What do these say?"

"That one states how much I have deposited at the Bank of England. The others list all the properties I own and their values. Improvements I want to make. In short, the ledgers are a reckoning of my entire fortune and my future plans to increase it."

A fortune in information if one knew how to take advantage of that.

While Fanny collected the ledgers from the bed into a neat pile, Jeremy went to inspect the lock on the door, because it had slowly opened itself again without help.

He studied the latch and wood, then swore under his breath. "It's been forced open," he said to her in a whisper. "I can't secure it again, either. Come, gather up your valuables and we'll inform the duke."

"Not tonight. I don't want to worry Papa before the wedding."

Fanny was rifling through the small case Jeremy had brought to Stapleton for her. And then she went through the contents a second time.

"Worry him? For heaven's sake, Fanny, nothing material might be stolen, but your right to privacy under your father's roof has been. You must tell him."

She paused finally in her frantic search. "Oh dear."

"What?"

"Our agreement. It was in the satchel this morning, and now it's no longer there."

Jeremy narrowed his eyes on her. He hadn't really read the agreement. He couldn't actually read more than a few words, but Lady Rivers had not known that when she'd insisted he sign it. She'd told him enough that he'd been grateful; to have someone take an interest in his career and give him a little in the way of funds was more then he'd hoped for. "Are you sure you haven't simply misplaced it?"

"No, it was definitely inside this journal." She covered her mouth and stared at him a long time. "This is a nightmare."

"Why?" Jeremy drew closer to Fanny, curious about her panic. "Our arrangement shouldn't cause an embarrassment for you. Other actors have wealthy patronesses support them all the time and no one seems to care very much."

"Yes," she whispered. "But with you it's different."

That made him smile but he shook aside the sense of pride. "Now about your father…"

"Tomorrow. I'll need you to stay with me again tonight," she asked, looking up at him slowly. "If the door will not lock, I simply won't be able to close my eyes wondering if whoever it was will come back."

"Stapleton will want to know about this," he persisted.

"I'd rather deal with this matter without his help."

Jeremy could see her heels digging in. She was worried, but not enough in his opinion. "Why won't you tell him what has transpired?"

"Because he'll only worry and then he'll wake every one of the guests to question them. We would run the risk of starting a scandal that I'd very much like to avoid. The state the room was left in makes me wonder if a scandal was what was hoped for. Father's enough on his mind now with the wedding, Gillian and the death of Mr. Hawthorne. I will not risk ruin of my sister's wedding. This must be a happy occasion. Trust me, my problem can wait a few days."

"Why have you not used your safe for storing your papers? Isn't that customary for someone like you?"

Fanny winced. "I lost the only key years ago."

Jeremy sighed. He could help her open it tonight. To an untrained eye, the location of the safe wasn't obvious. But he'd gleaned its location immediately. Behind the painting that was being blocked from view by the dressing screen. He pretended ignorance. "I might be able to help. Where is it? The safe? Is it in this room?"

"Behind that painting over there." She gestured to the screened corner. "I don't suppose you know how to pick locks?"

He pulled a face, unhappy about the question. There were many aspects of his former life he'd prefer to keep from Fanny, but her immediate need exceeded his objection. "Yes, as a matter of fact I do, but don't tell anyone."

"How marvelous!" She hurried to the screen and pulled down the painting, revealing a style of safe he knew well. "I would be very grateful to have my safe open again. Did you learn for a role onstage?"

He stepped up to pretend to study the mechanism. It was a simple lock for a man of his special talents. He hadn't picked a lock in years, but he was sure not to have forgotten one bit of his training. "I'll need a hair pin and one of your longer hat pins."

Lady Rivers provided both and stepped back to observe.

Jeremy had the safe open in under half a minute. He moved back, keeping his face lowered to hide a flush of shame that had warmed his cheeks.

"You really are a clever fellow," Fanny enthused.

"There aren't many who'd think so if they'd seen me do that."

She darted to the open safe and thrust her hand inside. "At last, my pretty," she crooned. She held up a tiny necklace for Jeremy to see. "I thought I would never hold these again."

"They're pretty," Jeremy murmured. But also very ordinary.

Fanny smiled though. "They're only coral but they were my mothers, and I always intended to give them to my daughter. Perhaps I'll give them to one of my sisters' children instead."

Jeremy watched her coil them around her fingers, then he covered her hand holding the necklace. "You should keep them for your own daughter, or a granddaughter."

"If I had been blessed with children in my marriage, perhaps I might have reason. Now they are just a reminder that I'm alone."

"You don't have to be alone if you don't want to be," he said and then scoffed at himself. What right did he have to give her advice about making a second marriage?

She shook her head. "It wasn't meant to be. Are you sure you can open the lock again later?"

"Most assuredly. Why?"

"I'd like to be able to open it again."

"I won't have any trouble."

Fanny collected her jewels and placed them all inside.

"There's enough room to put your ledgers inside, too, if you want," Jeremy noted.

"I've never kept those anywhere but with me or under my mattress when I travel."

He rolled his eyes. "Not exactly the safest place."

"It was when I only invited gentlemen I trusted into my bedchamber."

He met her gaze and felt both pleasure and a touch of exasperation. Fanny was definitely too trusting. "Humor me on this, my lady. Keep all your important papers in a safe from now on."

"Oh, all right, if you insist." She fetched the ledgers herself and plopped them in with her horde of jewels and stood back. "Are you sure you can close and open the safe again?"

"Not in any doubt, but only when you ask me to," he promised.

Since there was no key, Jeremy manipulated the lock with the pins to lock it again. Fanny peered over his shoulder as he made sure the door was secure.

She put her hand on his arm. "What was the

part you had to play that made you learn to pick locks?"

"I don't remember," he lied, and then hated himself for needing to do so. Picking locks should have no part in his current life. It was dangerous work with dangerous consequences. "I would appreciate it if you did not tell your father of my skills with locks."

"I wasn't going to," she promised. "Besides, I like knowing little secret things about you that no one else does."

He didn't. He felt exposed and ashamed every single time she managed to squeeze out some unsavory detail of his poor past. He finally faced her. "Now about your door." Jeremy stared at her. "How about a compromise?"

"What sort of compromise?"

"The kind where I don't spend the night here again. Barricade the door with furniture instead."

Fanny glanced about the chamber unhappily. "But every piece of furniture is too heavy for me to move without making a noise and drawing attention, which is the last thing I want to do at this hour."

Jeremy raked a hand through his hair. "I hadn't thought of that."

"Do you mind very much staying with me again?"

"Of course not." He shrugged away his concern for the proprieties. He could move about the house very silently if he put his mind to it, and he had a hundred well-considered excuses up his sleeve if he was spotted in the wrong place. But he didn't want to get back into the bad habit of skulking around houses that someone else owned. "I suppose it will only hurt the first time a member of your family murders me."

She laughed softly at his suggestion. "They'll understand why you stayed when I tell them why, after the wedding."

"Let's hope they are not under the influence when you do." He turned around, placing a chair directly in front of the door. "I was looking forward to continuing my part in your delightful country play."

"Not so delightful tonight I'm afraid."

"I've not had a turnip thrown at me yet." He lowered to sit in the chair, crossed his legs at the ankle and folded his arms over his chest. If anyone came to his lady's room tonight, Jeremy would deal with them. "Try to get some sleep."

Fanny was suddenly beside him, shaking his shoulder. "Are you not going to sleep beside me again?"

He glanced up at her in surprise. Last night had been an aberration, a product of grief renewed and convenience that he was around. "I'm guarding you."

She licked her lips. "Well, but, yes, so… You could also protect me from the comfort of my bed, too."

Jeremy looked at the bed, and then at the door,

and then at Fanny standing there with her plump bottom lip caught between her teeth. He knew where he'd rather sleep.

"Please," she whispered. "I would feel better for having you near, and you need your rest for tomorrow, too."

Jeremy carefully propped the delicate chair against the door on two legs, nudging the back under the handle and making sure it would stay there. It wouldn't stop anyone from entering the chamber if they put their back into shoving the door. But any movement of the chair should wake him. "If anyone comes during the night, get under your bed and leave the cur to me."

"I will," she promised. "I feel safer already just knowing you'll be here to confront anyone that comes." Fanny slipped behind her dressing screen, apparently not needing his help to change tonight.

He grew warm just thinking about those delicious curves he'd held last night. His hands itched to hold her, and his mouth grew dry because he *did* want to kiss her properly just once before he returned to London.

Thankfully, Fanny returned quickly, attired in the same prim nightgown but with a robe over the top. She moved to her mirror to take down her hair from the tight coils she'd had it styled in for dinner.

Jeremy sucked in a breath as she unwound the strands and ran her fingers through the long locks to the ends.

Fanny turned to him. "Is something wrong?

He took a step in her direction. "Where I grew up, women only grew their hair long to sell it."

She beamed. "Would you like to touch it?"

He nodded and crossed the room to her side, his fingers itching to become tangled up in the softness of a pampered head of hair. He drew some up to his face to brush across his cheek, but was startled by a memory dredged up from the murky depths of his past. "I think my mother had hair almost as long as yours."

"I thought you said you didn't remember her?"

He shook his head. "I don't really. But this reminded me that her hair was long and brown."

"Like yours."

"Prettier." He backed away. Too much intimacy between them was dangerous. He was playing a role and not meant to forget his purpose in being here. "You should get some rest. Tomorrow will be another emotional day, I suspect."

She gathered her hair together and tied it loosely with a ribbon at her nape. She dabbed sweet-smelling cream to her face and neck and then suddenly turned to face him. "I'm glad you remembered your mother. I think she'd be proud of her son."

"Not if she could see where I'm standing." Jeremy threw an arm wide, gesturing her toward her bed impatiently. "Good night, Lady Rivers."

Fanny climbed into her bed and then patted the space beside her. "Come to bed, Jeremy."

Jeremy hesitated a moment before joining her. Tonight, though, he kept his jacket and boots on. He wanted nothing to impede his speed if someone came back…or when he snuck out of the chamber a second night in a row.

But sleep eluded him. He was alert to every creak of the great house around them.

Fanny, he believed, remained wide awake on her side of the bed, too. Her feet kept shifting, her occasional sigh loud in the dark room.

He turned his head to face her. "Did you sleep beside your husband when you were married?"

Fanny rolled toward him. "Yes."

"How did you sleep? In his arms or separated?"

"Why do you want to know that?"

"Well, I don't really have a specific reason other than distracting you from worrying that someone might return." He shrugged. "And if I was ever to be offered the role of a loving husband in a play, I merely wondered what my options would be for the bedroom scene."

She sighed. "Not all husbands like to share a bed with their wives. Even when they love them to distraction."

He nodded. "What sort of man should I be? Someone who holds you all night long or worships from afar?"

"This is just a play we are speaking of, isn't it?"

He drew in a slow breath. He wanted to hold

her tonight very much, but he was waiting for her to at least hint in that direction, too. "Of course. I am yours to direct."

Fanny shifted closer and when he lifted his arm, she curled up to his side. The scent of her body, the cosmetic she's smoothed over her skin, did nothing to calm his rapidly beating heart. He glanced at the ceiling as his cock began to thicken. It had last night, too, though he'd had better success in willing it away.

Fanny sighed softly. "This is perfect."

"It is," he agreed. Jeremy kept his arm loose about her back, fighting the need to draw her closer still. "But it must be for the last time."

"I'm sure it will be," she promised and then yawned, burrowing against his chest. She looked up suddenly. "What sort of a person carries around a turnip only to throw it onto a performer on stage?"

He laughed softly against her hair. "I've no idea or desire to learn, my lady."

"Fanny. I like hearing you say my name."

"Fanny," he whispered.

Jeremy knew the precise moment Fanny fell asleep soon after. The sound of her even breaths filled his ears and soothed him in ways he didn't quite understand. He'd never had this with any woman before. The holding, the laughing, the falling asleep together, confiding in each other.

He glanced down at her face. In sleep, as she

was when awake, Fanny was stirringly beautiful but so far out of his reach.

He allowed himself to imagine for a moment a future where he would always have Fanny in his arms. But he shouldn't delude himself that she really needed him. He was a convenient distraction…just like all her other strays had been before he'd come along.

Chapter Nine

Fanny added the last flower to her sister's hair and stood back. "What do you think?"

"I think she looks beautiful," Jessica gushed.

"Indeed," Gillian, the Duchess of Stapleton, agreed. "Rafferty will be the one to swoon today, I think."

Rebecca smiled but shook her head. "He would never swoon. Besides, he needs to stay on his feet to speak his vows. He can swoon all he likes after we are man and wife, preferably not while he's carrying me over the threshold of his bedchamber."

Fanny scoffed at the idea of such a dangerous lapse in concentration on Rafferty's part. "It would never happen."

Rebecca's gown for the wedding was a delicate pink silk. The low neckline was almost scandalous to wear for a wedding but then again…this wasn't Rebecca's first marriage, and everyone knew the couple was deeply in love.

Fanny wore blue, Jessica rose, and the duchess wore pale green. She picked up the posy of flowers that Rebecca would carry, delivered by Whitfield fresh from his garden a few moments ago. "You'll be needing this."

"Indeed, I will," Rebecca agreed, standing and fluffing out her skirts. "Oh, I would give anything to have this part over and done with quickly. I hate being gawked at."

"We know," they all said in unison.

"But today you must accept your place as the center of attention and accept it as your due," the duchess murmured, coming closer to the jittery bride. "And well deserved it is. Rafferty told me only yesterday that he is quite the catch."

"So was Papa." Rebecca scowled. "Father deprived *you* of *your* due by marrying you in London by special license and not inviting more than a handful."

Gillian shrugged. "But I've been gawked at ever since the news spread around. You're well known in society so the gawking will cease very soon, I'd expect, as people accept that you are both happy. Whereas the novelty of my marriage to your father seems determined to endure forever."

To Fanny's surprise, Rebecca captured Gillian's hand. "They gawk because you are so beautiful and smile so often."

"Thank you. Loving your father does that," Gillian promised, a blush brightening her cheeks.

"He needed you," Rebecca insisted with a soft smile.

Fanny blinked several times in shock as the exchange continued. What an alteration love had brought to her sister's attitudes in recent weeks. Rebecca had been against Gillian right from the outset of her arrival at Stapleton. Vocally so. Now, though, the pair seemed almost the best of friends.

"I had better go take my place with the guests and have Nicolas waiting to collect you from the hall," Gillian whispered. "I'll see you all downstairs."

"Could you take Jessica with you and tell father I'll be delayed a few more minutes. I'd like to speak with Fanny alone if you don't mind."

Jessica, always agreeable, kissed Rebecca's cheek and left with Gillian.

Fanny cocked her head when they were gone. "What did you want to talk to me about at a time like this?"

"Nothing." Rebecca looked up at the ceiling and let out a long sigh. "I just needed a minute and used talking to you as an excuse."

Fanny didn't mind but she was curious. "Having doubts?"

"About Rafferty? No," she sighed. "He's been wonderful."

"What then?"

Rebecca glanced down at her posy. "In a few minutes, my whole life will change. I will no longer be Mrs. Rebecca Warner."

"Widow of a heartless scoundrel who betrayed you with his housekeeper right under her nose?" Fanny suggested, getting to the humiliating truth straight away rather than sugarcoating it. Rebecca usually preferred that.

"Yes." Rebecca shook her head. "I have to let it

all go. My anger and mistrust. I need to reinvent myself as Adam's countess."

Fanny put her arm about Rebecca's shoulders. "I hate to be the one to tell you this, but you have already changed in so many ways because of him and love. You are different already. Less offended by men."

"I worry."

Fanny knew her sister well. "That he'll turn away to another love?"

Rebecca chewed her lip and then nodded.

"Adam and your late husband are so dissimilar it is impossible to imagine it could happen. Rafferty adores you. Always wears a smile when you are around. If he should ever stray, or you were to give up on him, I would give up my fortune and go live in a hay field and wear rags."

"Well, I cannot have that." Rebecca chuckled. "My favorite sister must always be the most elegant woman in the room. *I insist* upon that."

Fanny moved to stand behind Rebecca as she stood before an arc of mirrors. She put her arm around Rebecca again, the way she had often done when they were younger. "The gown becomes you. Makes you seem a young bride again."

"I was happy then."

Fanny gave her a squeeze. "But not as much in love as I suspect you are now. Why, you are positively radiant."

Rebecca's eyes flashed to hers through the

mirror's reflection and held for a long minute. "You know, don't you?"

Fanny winked. "I cannot *know* anything until I'm told. Officially."

Rebecca's hand slipped to her belly where Fanny's hands still rested over a small bump.

Fanny chuckled softly. "That's how I know you and Adam will endure. You would never have allowed Warner the same liberties before you married him."

"No. I wouldn't have. I wanted to be, tried to be…freer. A little bit more like you."

"Like me?"

"Freer with my affections. Less concerned with the consequences of a dalliance as you have been."

"I have no dalliances, Rebecca."

"We share a bedchamber wall, sister." Rebecca's brow lifted. "You can confide in me, you know. I would never tell."

"There's nothing *to* tell," she promised, drawing away from her sister. Surely a dalliance required a kiss. Jeremy hadn't even tried. "Are you ready to wed now, Becca dear?"

"We're talking." Rebecca shook her head. "Rivers would understand."

Fanny frowned. She didn't want to have this conversation, but Rebecca seemed disinclined to let the matter drop. "You know why I will not marry."

"I'm not speaking of marriage. The idea is ludicrous, unless you want that. But the future is easier to face with someone to hold you when you are lonely. There's no good reason to deny yourself the warmth of a human connection out of fear they might die one day. Everyone needs hope. Affection. Perhaps a little lovemaking."

Fanny gaped. "I cannot believe you just said that to me."

"I can hardly keep to the moral high ground when I'm about to marry a man like Rafferty," Rebecca complained. "He's opened my eyes and assaulted my ears with all manner of indelicate conversation. The odd thing is, I don't even seem to mind anymore. As long as it's not *his* exploits with other women I hear about, I am content to let society be as scandalous as it pleases. That includes you and our brothers, too."

"I think I must already love Rafferty like a brother for bringing about this change in you." Rafferty wasn't a prude, and his relaxed morality was already rubbing off on her often-too-serious sister. "He will make an excellent addition to the family."

"Yes. Oh, and speaking of additions, that reminds me. Rafferty heard that the Thwaite family finances are under additional strain. The son, Wilks, is rumored to have run up gambling debts all over Town. Thwaite is trying to keep it quiet."

Fanny frowned. "Lord Thwaite is seeking out investors for a new venture."

"Yes, I thought you said something to that

effect a few nights ago. Will it make a difference not to have him involved or his funds in it?"

"Without him… Yes, it definitely could." It might be nothing but gossip, but Fanny would make sure of Thwaite's involvement before she made her final decision on the project. "He was very keen to have me agree to invest but I put him off until after the wedding." Fanny rushed to her sister's writing desk and scrawled a quick note to remind herself to investigate Thwaite's financial affairs more thoroughly in the morning.

She already suspected it had been him in her chambers, seeking information about the extent of her business dealings with Maxwell Danvers. And he might now have leverage to use against her in the future with regard to Jeremy Dawes, too. But she could not think of herself until after the wedding. She would never spoil her sister's happy day.

Rebecca clucked her tongue. "Come on, Fanny. Rafferty will start to think that I'm not coming down to marry him. You're making me late."

"I wasn't the one dragging her feet," Fanny reminded Rebecca as she slipped the note into her glove for safekeeping until she could return to her room later that day.

"Well, I can't blame myself," Rebecca said with a haughty expression. "What would people say if they thought I had any doubts?"

Fanny threw up her hands in resignation and

hurried to beat Rebecca out the door, managing to slip into the hall ahead of her to hold out her arm. "Shall we?"

"Indeed, we shall."

They moved briskly toward the staircase but started down more slowly.

Before too long, they heard the low murmur of dozens of voices from the drawing room. Father was pacing the hall.

"Finally," he cried when he spotted them descending, but then his face went soft and adoring. "Becca."

"Hello, Papa. How do I look?"

His eyes filled with emotion. "So much like your mother that for a moment, I thought you were her come back to life."

Fanny's own eyes welled with happy tears to hear that, but she quickly dashed them away. Rebecca was the only one who resembled their mother in any fashion.

She even had her volatile temper.

A footman was waiting at the doorway and, at Father's signal, the man stamped his cane on the floor to announce them. The crowd inside was immediately silenced.

Father bent to murmur in Rebecca's ear, whispering something meant for her alone. Fanny turned away to give them privacy, experiencing a touch of resentment, too.

Fanny's wedding day had been darkened because her father had not truly approved her choice the first time. Perhaps that was why from time to time he suggested she reconsider her solitary life but married to someone he approved of. She could be happily married if she wanted to be. If she ever found a good man, someone she could trust, she might consider it one day. But all the gentlemen she had encountered in society since becoming a widow were not remotely interesting and coveted her fortune.

She moved to the doorway and paused, taking stock and smiling at everyone assembled in the drawing room looking back at her. There were lords and ladies, locals, and many who had traveled to honor the couple on this special day.

People had traveled miles for her, too, and she'd loved every moment of the fuss.

But it was no wonder Rebecca had been nervous about today. This was the biggest wedding that Stapleton Manor had ever hosted, including Fanny's and Jessica's.

From the corner of her eye, she spotted Jeremy Dawes standing at the back of the room. The sight of him, so handsome, so appealing, made a flush of warmth—lust, if she were honest with herself—sweep over her skin.

She had to admit she'd like a kiss from him… and maybe quite a bit more besides, if he was agreeable.

Fanny squared her shoulders when Rebecca murmured her name, and she swept down between the rows of guests toward Lord Rafferty and the waiting vicar.

It would be some hours now before she was released from family obligations. Perhaps by that time she'd have relegated her longing for masculine company to the back of her mind again.

She moved to the side, ready and willing to be a witness to the nuptials about to take place.

She lifted her face to see her sister approach. Any trace of pre-wedding nerves had vanished from Rebecca's demeanor. She was radiant again as she took the groom's hand, and Rafferty's face was so full of love it was hard to witness. Father nodded to her as he took his seat beside his new wife.

As the vicar spoke, Fanny was constantly reminded of her own distant wedding day. She had loved her husband dearly, until his last breath and beyond. But she had to admit that her life felt so empty of late. The work she did for the poor, managing her investments, helping the family when she could, did not satisfy her as much as it once had.

Perhaps she *did* need someone in her life from time to time.

Not a husband, surely. A temporary companion only. A husband would take over her financial affairs and leave her life emptier than it was now. Perhaps Rebecca was right, that an affair with a discreet lover might just be what she needed. For now, Dawes was an amusing companion, and she was enjoying their little performances together.

Rafferty slipped a ring on Rebecca's finger and the pair were wed.

They turned to face the wedding guests as man and wife to wild applause from family and guests.

Fanny thanked the vicar and fell in behind them, standing beside Wilks as the guests swamped the grinning couple.

"Lady Rivers, how lovely to see you again," he drawled.

"And you as well, my lord."

"When are we going to do something together?" Wilks and Fanny had different friends and rarely moved in the same circles. "I don't know."

"I was talking about *doing*," he waggled his brows suggestively, "*something. Together.* After all, my best friend and your sister *are* now wed. We should become better *friends,* don't you think?"

Fanny nearly rolled her eyes at the emphasis Wilks placed on certain words. Did he think she was desperate for manly attention? Lord Wilks, being younger than her, would be the last man she'd ever allow into her bed. He was Thwaite's son and a libertine. She adopted her most haughty expression. "I don't follow."

"Well, Rafferty is fond of a house party, and as I recall, you are too." He hooked her arm though his and patted her hand. "We could see *much* more of each other very easily."

"I *have* attended several house parties in recent years," she agreed. To discuss investments, and to keep boredom at bay. She'd not bed hopped at any of the prior ones that Wilks had attended. But she hadn't been looking for a lover then. She wasn't now, either. "I'm sure we will attend several of the same house parties in future years. That is unavoidable."

Jessica rushed over and caught hold of Fanny's upper arms, dislodging Wilks in the process with her enthusiasm. "Isn't it wonderful, Fanny?" Jessica cried out as she embraced her.

"What is wonderful?"

"How one wedding almost always leads to another," Jessica enthused. "I suppose you already know that Lord Letterford has proposed to Mrs. Abercrombie and been accepted. Why didn't you tell us when he must have told you at luncheon the other day?"

Fanny gaped and quickly looked around the room, discovering Lord Letterford and Mrs. Abercrombie, a widow close to his own age, standing not far away. "He never mentioned an attachment."

"She wears his ring even now." Jessica linked arms with her, turning her away from Wilks. "I cannot wait until dinner. There will be mushroom soup. My favorite."

Wilks faded into the mingling guests and Jessica let out a huff. "Eh, that man is horrible."

"I take it you've had dealings with Wilks before."

Her sister frowned. "I met him during my season. He was forever trying to talk to me alone. I talked to him about mushrooms for an hour before he lost interest."

Fanny laughed. "Well, I'm glad you were cautious around him."

"You should be too. There are much nicer men to choose from to marry than that one."

"Whoever said I was getting married?"

"Well, everyone. I'm always the last one to know."

"That is not true. You'll be first, I promise, should I even decide I miss having a husband to boss me around. Not that I do. Or have even considered the prospect of making a second match for myself."

Jessica was frowning. "I don't get bossed around!"

Whitfield was suddenly beside them. "Jessica, we should congratulate the happy couple. Now, while there's no one close to them."

"See?" Fanny muttered under her breath as Whitfield led Jessica away. A husband would tell her what to do just like Whitfield was with Jessica now, and Fanny had grown rather fond of bossing herself about instead.

Fanny made her way to Lord Letterford and Mrs. Abercrombie. "My dears, I just heard the happy news. Congratulations. How simply wonderful!"

"Thank you, my lady," Mrs. Abercrombie said with a loving glance toward Letterford. "We wanted to wait till after the wedding, but Letterford couldn't hold his tongue."

"And so he shouldn't have."

"Thank you, Fanny," Letterford murmured with a small smile. "I say, would now be a good time for us to discuss that spot of business I mentioned before? It will only take a moment, I swear."

Since Fanny had thought Letterford was going to embarrass himself and her by proposing, she was taken by surprise that he still wanted to talk to her. "Oh, yes. If you like."

"Excuse me, my dear. I will be right back," he promised Mrs. Abercrombie.

He took Fanny away from everyone. "Forgive my deception, but I wanted to ask a favor and I hope you won't think I am presuming on our long acquaintance to ask, but," he seemed to gulp, "I wonder if I might have the use of your house in Brighton? You see, Mrs. Abercrombie has never seen the sea. I'd like to take her there for our honeymoon trip for a few weeks after we marry."

Fanny smiled warmly. "You may visit and stay as long as you like. I'll send word to the housekeeper today to expect to hear from you soon, and when you'll be arriving."

"That is good of you." He gulped. "How much might you want—"

Fanny silenced him with a wave of her hand. "My wedding gift to you both."

"I couldn't possibly accept."

Letterford wasn't a wealthy man, and a late marriage like his deserved the best start possible. "You must accept, because *I* will not accept a penny in payment," she warned.

"You are far too generous. Thank you so much." He smiled shyly. "It is my fervent hope that one day you find a gentleman who regards you as highly as you deserve, too."

"Thank you, and the best of luck to you both." She waved him off, back to his intended bride.

Jeremy appeared at her side, his expression thoughtful. "What did Letterford want with you?"

"Nothing I wasn't happy to give," she promised with a laugh and then twined her arm though Jeremy's. She had one less man to avoid now and that made her day so much brighter. "It's a wonderful wedding, isn't it?"

Chapter Ten

Jeremy was surprised to discover he seemed to be a tasty treat on the menu for a number of the female guests at the wedding. He hadn't been so manhandled since he'd tried to slip in to see his first play. The women of the *ton* were utterly shameless in the way they winked, stared and rubbed up against him as the evening fell, along with their inhibitions. They assumed he could have no objections to their fumbling fingers and suggestive offers to meet later in some out-of-the-way spot.

But they didn't know he wasn't about to break out of character for anyone.

At the wedding breakfast, Jeremy had unfortunately been seated away from Fanny—too far away to even see the bridal party at the other end of the room. He missed having someone he could talk to.

"Are you all right there, Dawes?" the duke asked, suddenly appearing at his elbow with a drink in hand.

"I am, your grace," he promised quickly

"Despite your face saying otherwise," Stapleton murmured.

Jeremy turned to the duke and kept his voice

low. "Did your daughter by chance speak with you yet?"

"Which daughter? I do have three."

"Your eldest."

"We said good morning and then she said go away. Apparently, my opinion wasn't wanted earlier in the day. Ladies only," he confided. "Why?"

"Ah," Jeremy murmured, floundering for a moment. He guessed Fanny hadn't told him about her bedchamber being ransacked yet. She really should have. "I'm sure she'll find a moment to speak with you later tonight."

The duke gave him a long considering look. "It *would* save time if you'd just spit it out."

"No. She wouldn't like that," Jeremy decided.

The duke huffed. "Daughters. They'll be the death of me, I swear."

Despite the seriousness of what had occurred last night, he couldn't help but chuckle at the duke's long face. "I'm sorry."

"I'm not. Women keep men on their toes." The duke sighed. "Well, if you're not going to inform on her, I'd better wait for her to come to me in her own time."

But how long would that be? Jeremy hoped not too long. He wouldn't be spending another night in her chambers, but at least he knew her door latch had been fixed and a secondary bolt added at his request, too.

The duke was pulled away and Jeremy was left standing alone again. Across the room, Fanny glided past on the arm of a friend of hers. She appeared to be having a marvelous time. She'd danced twice, though not with him. He probably should have asked but to be honest, his dancing skills were not quite good enough for public display.

A heavy hand landed on his shoulder. Jeremy turned, expecting that the duke had returned to plague him.

But it was Lord Wilks' smirking countenance in front of him instead. "She's a lovely sight, isn't she?"

"Who?"

"You know who. Lady Rivers is quite remarkable."

Jeremy had taken an immediate dislike to Wilks and it wasn't because he was three sheets to the wind already. There was just something decidedly too slick and false about his laugh to make Jeremy feel he was entirely trustworthy. "Yes, she is indeed," Jeremy murmured.

"Tell me, do you have to follow *all* her orders —I'm sorry, *stage directions*—like a pampered pug on a leash or does she let you be a man and take charge of her on occasion?"

Jeremy stared at the fellow in shock and not a little revulsion, too. "What nonsense are you talking about?"

"Oh, come now. You did well to convince her to sponsor your fledgling career on the stage, but surely you could have asked for much more than a token payment of a hundred pounds. You're pretending to be in love with her and deserve a higher compensation. She'd never have felt the pinch." Wilks threw his arm over Jeremy's shoulder. "I can help you squeeze more blunt out of her, for a modest fee, of course."

Jeremy was appalled at the suggestion but tried to keep his shock off his face. He threw Wilks' arm from his shoulders and faced the drunkard. How could Wilks have deduced their arrangement in one half day? He'd arrived barely in time for the nuptials, unless…

Unless he'd been given the agreement to read since the marriage had taken place.

Jeremy swore under his breath as he took in Wilks' smug countenance. Had Lord Thwaite stolen Jeremy's employment agreement from Fanny's chambers and shared the contents with his drunkard of a son? Obviously, Wilks intended to use that information to line his own pocket, too.

He glanced across the chamber, only to see Fanny slipping from the ballroom with her sisters in tow. There was no way he could warn her. The bride was about to head off to her new home, if he remembered correctly. It was the perfect moment for Wilks to approach him, when everyone's attention was diverted to the other side of the ballroom.

Jeremy steadied his temper. He couldn't become flustered over the conversation. He intended to get that piece of paper back to Fanny tonight.

Wilks patted his pocket. "I could certainly make it worth your while to reconsider where your loyalties lie."

Jeremy's eyes narrowed on Wilks. The contract was in his pocket, right in front of him.

He had vowed not to waste this once-in-a-lifetime opportunity, but his loyalty was to Fanny, not his own pocket. He smiled quickly, playing along with the fellow's scheme to make him seem amenable. "How much should I have asked for?"

"Meet me tomorrow in the orchard at noon, and we can discuss it," Wilks advised with another smirk.

Three booming rings from a staff upon the parquetry floor and Jeremy turned toward the sound. "Ladies and gentlemen, the Earl and Countess of Rafferty are taking their leave."

People applauded, and then surged toward the entrance hall to see the newlyweds off.

Jeremy was bumped hard in the rush to reach the doorway first, falling conveniently against Wilks. The man threw him off—but not before Jeremy had checked inside his coat pockets and lifted a paper he found there.

It felt about the same size as the brief contract he's signed. He had no time to check though. Jeremy palmed it as he righted himself, apologizing profusely, while he quickly flicked it up his coat sleeve and followed everyone else out the door.

Jeremy winced. His scandalous past had come in handy for his new role twice now. It would be the last time, too.

He followed everyone outside into the gathering gloom, suppressing the instinct to slip into the shadows to check what he'd pinched from Lord Wilks to make sure he had Fanny's property.

Fanny was down on the driveway by the carriage, surrounded by her family, dabbing at her eyes, brushing aside happy tears—at least he hoped they were happy. He'd noticed she seemed to cry all sorts of tears. He found that confusing, but he had a handkerchief ready in his hand in case it was needed.

The wedding guests gathered on the steps together as groom and blushing bride climbed into the carriage and finally drove away toward Lord Rafferty's home.

Fanny and Lord Thwaite fell into step on their way back inside. Thwaite was wearing a pleased expression, and he whispered something to Fanny that made her laugh. But she was quickly drawn away by the duchess and her remaining sister and swept into the house.

Jeremy put his hand to his coat pocket, returning his handkerchief.

The man in front of him turned about abruptly, and he found himself staring straight into Wilks' eyes again.

The fellow touched his pocket, and his eyes narrowed as he searched for something that was no longer in his possession. "What did you put in your coat pocket?" he demanded.

"What, my handkerchief?"

Wilks checked his own pockets again and then turned a furious glare at Jeremy. "Show me."

"It's just a handkerchief," he promised, revealing it. "You can have it if you require one."

But Wilks grabbed him roughly and tried to search Jeremy's coat pockets. Jeremy protested at the rough treatment as much as the stink of spirits on Wilks' breath, loudly.

"Get off me." Jeremy threw an arm out, connecting his fist with Wilks' jaw accidentally.

Wilks stumbled back a step, but he wasn't giving up. "Give it back!"

"What the hell is this?" Stapleton barked, stepping between them. "Gentlemen, control yourselves."

It took Lord Milo and Lord Samuel to hold Wilks back from attacking Jeremy again. Wilks pointed at Jeremy, accusing, "He has something of mine. I am sure of it."

Jeremy straightened his coat, checking the note was still safe up his shirt sleeve. "I have nothing belonging to you." But he had something belonging to Fanny, and he did not want to reveal it here.

The duke folded his arms across his chest and looked between them. "An accusation of theft is a serious matter. What is it you think he's taken?"

"I have no idea, your grace," Jeremy promised. "He's cup shot."

"Am not! That man has something of great value to me," Wilks insisted. But he looked around, taking note of their audience with blinking eyes. He straightened his coat and smoothed his hair, but since he could hardly stand still anymore, he gave credence to Jeremy's accusation that he didn't know what he was talking about. "I cannot say what it is but it is vital it is returned to me tonight," Wilks insisted. "Who is he, anyway? Just an actor."

"He is a guest," Stapleton noted. "Just as you are tonight."

Jeremy approached the duke, stopping as close to his side as he dared. He managed to drop the folded contract into Stapleton's gaping coat pocket without him realizing it. "I don't have anything that belongs to *him*, I swear."

The duke's eyes narrowed on Wilks. "An accusation of theft can be resolved easily right now. Mr. Dawes, would you have any objection to being searched a second time with substantially more dignity?"

Jeremy had nothing to hide anymore. "I have no objection."

The duke frisked him quickly, efficiently, thoroughly, even patting his shirt front a few times and arms to be sure he'd nothing stashed inside his clothing. Satisfied he carried no paper; the duke declared the accusation false and made them shake hands. "Wilks, you were wrong, and Mr. Dawes was provoked enough to defend himself. That is the end of it. Wilks, go sleep it off and cause me no more trouble."

However, the way Wilks glared at him alerted Jeremy that it wasn't over. The man's eyes almost glowed with hate. "Perhaps I misplaced it," Wilks conceded.

"I'll have my staff bring me anything they find." Then the duke turned to Jeremy, frowning. "Inside. My library. Now."

Jeremy complied, striding straight toward the duke's library with a confidence he didn't exactly feel. The duke was sure to follow, and then Jeremy would have to be damn quick to nick the contract back before Stapleton stuck his hand in his own pocket.

Fanny's brothers caught up to him as soon as he reached the library doorway. They drew him across the room to the decanters. "Nice little fight you had brewing there, Dawes, or would have been if Father hadn't interfered," Lord Samuel complained.

"Wilks could do with being taken down a peg or two," Lord Milo agreed, wearing a wide smirk of his own. Samuel poured port for the three of them. Milo, though, captured Jeremy's hand and inspected his knuckles. "No harm seems to be have been done."

"A pity some harm hadn't happened to Wilks' face," Samuel muttered. "He's traded off his looks and his title far too much in my opinion. No doubt someone will break that smirk off his face eventually. We were so hoping it would be you. What did Wilks want back?"

"I've no idea."

"Must be *some* love letter he's lost," Milo murmured, teasing perhaps. "Did you know Wilks ruined a business deal of our sisters last year? Seduced her previous maid to find out her plans before anyone. Not that we could prove it then. The way he's followed her about tonight leads me to think he's meddling with her life again, or his father has set him to it. And then I saw him talk to you tonight like old friends."

Jeremy frowned. "Why would Wilks seduce Fanny's maid and not Fanny?"

"Fanny is too smart to fall for false flattery or let down her guard around men coming courting. The maid was foolish in the extreme to trust any promises he made her." Milo pursed his lips. "Cost Fanny a fortune to unentangle herself from the project. But Fanny has a knack for turning everything things she touches into gold, so the loss was negligible in the end. She deserves better."

"Yes," Jeremy murmured.

Milo studied him. "We shouldn't like to see her wings clipped by any man in any marriage."

Jeremy agreed. "Nor would I. She is unlike any woman I've ever met."

He glanced down at his hand as his knuckles started to throb.

"You might want to get some ice for that." Milo nodded. "Ask the housekeeper to bind it, too. I'd better go mingle before Father sends me to a corner, too. He hates it when his children brawl."

Milo strolled from the room whistling and Jeremy was left alone with Samuel.

Jeremy turned to Samuel. "I thought the duke was coming to the library, too?"

"My father sends everyone to the library when he wants to cool his own temper." Samuel smiled and flicked up his fingers. Jeremy was astonished to see a folded piece of paper in his possession. "I'm thinking you'll be wanting this back."

Jeremy blinked. "Where did you get that?"

Samuel smiled as he unfolded it and appeared to read it rapidly. "From my father's own pocket. I possess none of your unique skills at picking pockets, but I have a habit of hugging him still, so…*voilà*. Well done pinching back Fanny's paper from Wilks. How on earth did he get hold of it?"

Jeremy wet his lips. "Why do you think it's Fanny's?"

"The paper and handwriting is hers. She writes all her family correspondence on the same sheets, too. Also, it's signed by her…and you. A fascinating arrangement you have here." Samuel passed it over. "You should really keep something so sordid under lock and key. People could misunderstand."

Jeremy began to feel uneasy about that

contract. What else was in it that he hadn't understood? "I will."

Lord Samuel inclined his head and turned about, heading for the exit.

Jeremy followed more slowly, stuffing the note inside his shirt. Samuel had already disappeared when Jeremy paused in the front hall. He did not want to return to the ball with the contract in his possession, certainly Lord Wilks lurked about and would watch for another chance to frisk him.

He turned for the stairs.

"Mr. Dawes!"

He shut his eyes briefly, wishing Fanny hadn't come looking for him. He turned politely though and saw Thwaite lurking at her side again. "Lady Rivers. Lord Thwaite."

She wet her lips. "We wondered where you'd gone. I heard…"

He thrust out his hand to show her his knuckles were only barely marked. "It was a misunderstanding. I was just on my way to get some assistance from the housekeeper."

Fanny caught his hand in hers and peered at his reddened knuckles, wincing. "How bad is this?"

"Stings a bit but Milo feels nothing is broken."

She sighed in relief. "I'm very glad to hear it."

Thwaite smirked, eyes sliding to Fanny. "I assured Lady Rivers that there's no ill feeling on my son's part either. The duke settled the matter. Wilks had a bit too much to drink. Besides, a bit of competition between young men over a lady's affections is good to see, especially when so great a prize is at stake."

Fanny's eyes dropped and he saw she was uncomfortable with the comment. Did she know Thwaite had taken their agreement, and passed it off to his son? Perhaps she did, or perhaps it was only the talk of winning her favor that bothered her. "My lady, might I have a private word with you?" he asked.

Thwaite held out his arm impatiently. He might as well have snapped his fingers, for the action caused Jeremy's hackles to rise. No man should treat Fanny that way. She belonged to no one but herself. "I'm afraid your word will have to wait. Lady Rivers has agreed to dance with me next, and then my son."

Her smile was brittle. "Yes. Indeed."

Jeremy took a step in her direction. "It will only take a moment."

She seemed torn but shook her head. Her face never rose to his as she whispered, "If you would excuse me. I must go."

She gathered up her skirts and headed into the ballroom with a grinning Thwaite following closely behind. Jeremy moved down one step, keen not to lose sight of her.

"It's fascinating that my family continues to associate with that slimy bastard," Samuel said as he emerged from the shadows of a nearby chamber. "Don't fret about m'sister. I'll keep an eye on her for you tonight. Get that hand looked at and leave Thwaite and his lecherous son to me. And for heaven's sake, put that piece of paper in a safer place than where they must have found it the first time."

Startled by his accurate assessment of the problem, Jeremy nodded and started up the stairs. Once he was in the dubious safety of his chamber, he fished the agreement out of his pocket. Squinting at it by moonlight, he tried to make sense of it for the next hour. But the task defeated him. He nearly crumpled it in frustration. He simply had to find someone trustworthy to read it to him…but who to trust in this place escaped him. The best person for the task was Fanny, but then she would find out he could not read.

And with Thwaite and Wilks hovering about her, he likely couldn't ask until tomorrow.

He glared at the paper. The best time to return the agreement to Fanny's chambers was probably now. He could slip into her chambers, open the safe, and lock the agreement away with none the wiser.

Chapter Eleven

Fanny hugged her brother Samuel's arm tightly as they strolled through the woods between the tall trees after calling upon Mrs. Hawthorne. The duke had impressed upon every single family member his desire to make a large show of respect for his departed friend who would be buried that very day. Everyone had ditched breakfast forks to accommodate his request for their participation in the visit. Everyone with sense and a desire for another invitation to spend time at Stapleton had kept their complaints about the early hour strictly to themselves, too.

The family was now officially in mourning for their friend and neighbor, and a great many of the guests would be leaving today.

Especially Lord Wilks and his father, Lord Thwaite. Wilks was a pest, and Thwaite kept trying to get her agreement to talk to her alone. Thanks to her brother's continued presence around her last night, Thwaite had never had a chance.

But earlier in the evening, Thwaite had made it plain that he had the agreement she'd signed with Dawes in his possession. He'd *found* it lying around, he'd claimed. He was prepared to have it returned to her today before he and his son departed.

Fanny expected to be blackmailed during the meeting.

But it would be Wilks who would meet with her to do the deed. She was suspicious of that, and was preparing herself for a demand of money to buy his silence as well.

She looked up at Samuel when he sighed heavily. His brow was drawn in lines of concentration. "What's the matter with you today?"

"Nothing really."

She hugged his arm again. "Is everyone pestering you to remarry as much as they are me?"

"It is as relentless as ever," he noted. "Do they have nothing better to think about?"

"I fear not. I thought I had become adroit at changing the subject until yesterday," Fanny murmured. "Yesterday's entreaties to wed sorely tested my patience with everyone. Some bordered on desperate. I had no idea so many of our acquaintances had younger sons in need of a wife's fortune to prop up their family's situations. I mean, of course I'd gladly sacrifice my own happiness to dig them out of troubles of their own making."

Samuel chuckled softly. "So, no chance of a wedding for you then?"

"No one who claims to love me, loves my fortune less."

Samuel threw his arm around her shoulders. "Fools, all of them. Your greatest assets have always been your heart, and your intellect."

Fanny hugged her brother back. "It is the way the world works, I'm sorry to say. There isn't a man alive who doesn't believe my fortune would be more capably managed in his hands than mine."

"I don't think that," Samuel protested.

"You have to say that because you're my brother. I'd never speak to you again if you thought me inferior to any man."

"Never would I want that," he grinned. "I'm sure there are many men who would give you your head in marriage. Not Wilks, of course, but your Mr. Dawes doesn't seem to object to being ordered about."

She tensed. "That is different."

"It must be quite the novelty that he's not exactly fawning all over you. I like him all the more for it."

"Yes, he does seem unimpressed by wealth," she said, feeling a renewed sense of disappointment that she'd ended up sleeping alone last night. The additional lock she'd not asked for had ensured no one could have entered her chamber. But Jeremy had left the party well before the festivities had truly reached their height. She had hoped he might come back down after his hand had been looked at, but he'd retired. She had wanted to ask about his fight with Wilks. "I have high hopes for him, as I've had for every other soul I've sought to help on their way to a better future."

"Your charity work is admirable but one day it's going to get you into trouble," Samuel warned.

"That is what *he* said, too."

"So, this connection you've begun with Dawes. Was it his idea or yours?"

She shrugged. "Mine, of course."

"Why not someone of our class? Surely there's someone you know who would share your bed without getting paid for it."

Fanny froze. "He has not shared my bed."

Samuel looked at her sideways. "That's not what your contract with him suggests."

Fanny looked at her brother with a sinking feeling. If Samuel knew, then Father knew. She was surprised he hadn't given her another scolding, even if she was too old for them now. "How did you—"

"A better question to ask is how Wilks got his slimy fingers on your private papers?"

She didn't say but closed her eyes. "Wilks showed you the contract. What did he ask of you?"

"Wilks asked me for nothing, but I take it he and his father are attempting to blackmail you over it, given their behavior toward you last night."

She nodded quickly. "I am to meet with Wilks today before he and his father leave, to retrieve the contract. I have no doubt he'll present me with a list of demands for his silence and a bill to pay. Don't worry, I can handle him myself."

"You don't know yet? *Devil take it.*" Samuel looked about frantically. "You must speak to Dawes before your meeting with Wilks takes place."

"Why? I don't need his help or any man's." Fanny stared at her brother. He was usually the least excitable of all her siblings but not at this moment.

"You do now," Samuel pulled her off the path to whisper, "The only thing Thwaite and Wilks have is an empty threat."

Fanny gripped her brother's arm. "How?"

"Ask Dawes. I can see now why you might want to keep him around." Samuel grinned. "Most proper gentleman wouldn't be able to pick a pocket as easily as he did last night and get away with it."

"*Picking pockets!?* No, he couldn't have done that."

"Saw it with my own eyes." Samuel nodded enthusiastically. "Very impressive. One day I must ask him to show me how it's done. You know how I love charlatans and thieves."

Fanny looked around for Jeremy too, now, but he seemed to have fallen far behind in the procession leading back to Stapleton Manor. She turned back to Samuel. "I can't see him. Can you?"

Samuel, much taller than Fanny, rose up on his toes. "No, I can't, actually. Strange. I wonder what's become of him."

A feeling of dread settled in her stomach. What

if Wilks had found him to finish what he'd started last night?

She had to find Jeremy immediately. She glanced around again and saw that everyone on their walk had caught up.

Since there was no sign of Jeremy, she grabbed her father's arm when he drew level to find out what he knew. "Papa, what has become of Mr. Dawes?"

"He's behind," Father said, looking back then, too. "Now, where the devil has that boy disappeared to? He was just there a moment ago."

She craned her neck, but she and Father were the last in the procession now. Samuel had fallen back into the line with everyone else. "When exactly did you see him?"

Father scratched his jaw. "I'm sure we spoke in the woods. He asked about the age of a tree, of all things. Perhaps he paused to rest there."

Fanny pressed her lips together momentarily. "I'll go back and fetch him. I'll join you all for luncheon shortly."

"Don't be too long." Father pointed to the horizon. "That'll be a nasty storm I should think when it finally arrives."

"Then I'd better hurry and find him." Fanny hitched up her skirts and rushed back along the path until she reached the trees. It was dark and gloomy inside the woods now, thanks to the approaching storm, and Jeremy might have gotten himself turned around. She should have kept a closer eye on him. The city-bred actor hardly knew his way around the manor and gardens, let alone a dark wood.

"Mr. Dawes," she called and stepped deeper into the gloom, listening intently for an answer. "Jeremy Dawes, show yourself."

Silence.

Taking one last look at the approaching dark skies, Fanny continued into the wood, glancing left and right of the trail. Jeremy had been wearing a moss-green coat today, which would make him exceptionally hard to see against the color of the forest surrounds.

Fanny had gone halfway back to the Hawthornes when she finally spotted him.

He was sitting upon an old tree stump to one side of the path. Legs crossed. Posture relaxed. Unworried by his isolation.

"Mr. Dawes," she cried out much louder than she needed to.

He startled and searched for her. "Fanny! What the devil are you doing here?"

"Looking for you." Fanny rushed to him. "What are you doing sitting there like that on the old tree stump? You had me so worried."

She sounded to her own ears like a mother scolding a child, and Fanny was definitely not that to Jeremy Dawes. She made an effort to calm herself.

"I didn't mean to worry you," he swore. He glanced around the wood and sighed. "I was just sitting here thinking that I've never been anywhere that I could be so entirely alone in my whole life."

She blinked. "I beg your pardon."

He stood up on the stump. "When I was a child, there were other orphans like me where I lived. We shared a straw corner, a cup for water, food. Punishments too. We were all walking along in a line today, as I had to do as a child sometimes at the orphanage, and I just stopped dead in my tracks. I didn't even care that I'd be left behind. I was happy to be alone. When I was young, that would have terrified me."

"Well, I would care if you'd been lost."

He smiled gently. Dismissively. "It's kind of you to say so."

She drew closer and thrust out her hand. "Come home with me now."

He looked around again. "I think I should like to live somewhere like this."

"In the woods?"

He nodded slowly. "I like the peace and the quiet very much. I never thought I would care for it. *The country*. It's so different from anything I've ever known."

Fanny stretched her hand out a little more. "I think you will not care for it when your belly is empty and your fire will not catch alight because the wood was so damp. And what of your ambition to become a leading actor on London's greatest stage? There's no audience to flatter your performance here. Come down from there now and attend me."

He jumped down from the tree stump. "Every career has its challenges. But wouldn't this make the most wonderful stage to perform upon? Can you picture it? An elevated stage set among the trees over there and bench seats dotted between the old oaks over here. Footmen with trays handing out champagne and canapes to the audience."

"Father would never allow so many to trample through his woods." Fanny caught his hand and tugged hard. "You and I have something important to talk about, sir. About Lord Wilks."

His gaze fell upon her face, and a frown replaced his contented expression. "What was in that contract that everyone but me feels is scandalous?"

"I…" Fanny faltered, her cheeks heating.

He raised one brow. "Tell me?"

She shrugged. "I like to be prepared for all eventualities."

"And by *all* eventualities, you mean…"

Fanny wanted the earth to open up and swallow her whole. She was certain he'd read that part of the contract, but apparently in his enthusiasm to accommodate her request to be his patron, he had not read it properly. "I considered that there might be a possibility that our continued association might lead to sharing a bed. I wrote conditions and compensations into the contract."

He stared at her with a frown, no doubt

puzzling through what she'd said. "We *have* shared a bed. I've slept with you twice now."

"*Slept.* The contract goes into greater detail." She gulped. "If we became intimate for any length of time, I imposed a limit to that relationship. I was certain you had read that passage," she whispered when it seemed clear he really hadn't understood at all.

"No. I did not." He folded his arms over his chest. "So, you actually imagined that the natural course of your patronage was that I would make love to you."

"I did consider that it *could* happen if we found we liked each other enough."

"Huh," he said. He raked his hand over his short hair, frown set in place even more firmly now. "Well. That does explain most of what Wilks said to me."

"My brother Samuel knows, too."

"So Thwaite stole it, Wilks tried to take advantage and bribe me with it, and your younger brother has read it too, but the duke hasn't ordered my murder yet." His eyes widened and he shook his head. "At least no one can *prove* we've been intimate."

"My sister suspects I haven't been alone in my room the last few nights. But it doesn't matter. She won't say a word. Thwaite has read the contract and could use it against me. I'm not sure what Wilks wants."

"Your money." Jeremy shook his head. "But the

contract is secure in your safe with your jewels and journals again."

"Thank heavens." Fanny sagged against Jeremy, relieved beyond measure as she hugged him. "Thank you."

His hand swept up her arm, his fingers moving to the back of her neck and teasing into her hair. He bent his head toward hers and whispered, "All they have is their filthy imaginations now. I highly doubt anyone would believe them on the strength of their word alone."

"They could still cause trouble if they made a copy, which I fervently hope they did not consider." She bit her lip and looked up at Jeremy, studying his face a moment before asking the question she most wanted confirmed. "How did you get the original contract back from them? Samuel suggested that you picked Wilks' pocket."

Jeremy's hand dropped from her skin. "Did he, now? What else did Samuel say?"

"He said I should ask you for the particulars. Well?"

Jeremy took a step back and glanced sideways. Fanny had the uncomfortable feeling he was preparing to run. She put out her hand to him. "Please, we need to talk about this."

He glanced her way, his expression shuttered. "There were good reasons I refused to talk about my past. The truth will not allow you to trust me more. In fact, it should do the opposite."

Fanny took her time to consider everything he

was not telling her. In a way, he was confirming everything. Jeremy Dawes had been, was still perhaps, a *thief.*

But Jeremy had been in the presence of her valuables on several occasions and she couldn't credit that he was dangerous to her. She had not felt, nor did she feel now, that he would steal from her. In fact, his picking a pocket and a lock had been done to help her alone.

It would be irrational that she might hold that past, and his recent actions, against him in the face of the aid he'd given her. "I won't ask you to explain now, but I will ask again."

He looked surprised by her response.

Right then, a drop of water landed on his cheek, and he looked up with an oath tumbling from his lips.

Fanny did too, but all she saw was raindrops falling through the dark canopy and threatening to drench them if they did not move. "We must hurry back to the manor. There is a storm approaching."

Jeremy immediately put his arm around her waist. "I've been rained on before, but you should certainly not be out in it."

They turned for home, hurrying along side by side. But when they reached the edge of the forest it was clear the storm was upon them already. Rain had begun to fall in great sheets across the open field, and with such dark clouds rolling in, the rain could soon become heavier.

She turned to Jeremy before they stepped out in the worst of it, mulling over what she'd learned in the woods again. Everyone had things in their past they didn't like to talk about. She was no different. Jeremy could keep his secrets, provided they did not impact her own life. "We don't need to talk about what you did or have done before we met, unless you want to tell me."

His smile reappeared. "I appreciate that. You probably wouldn't enjoy the telling unless it were put in a play anyway."

Fanny gasped. "Don't you dare put any of that in writing before you tell me. I think we can both agree I made a mistake writing that agreement, and it is a risk we should not take again with our reputations."

"You'll have no argument from me, my lady." He removed his coat and held it over her head. "We'll just go on the way we were before."

Relief swept through her but then a rolling boom of thunder shook them both, and Fanny suddenly found herself wrapped tightly in Jeremy's embrace. She wasn't sure if she'd moved to him or he'd moved to her. All she knew was that in his arms was where she'd like to stay for a while. A good long while. Jeremy felt very safe, even if he was a thief.

They looked at each other a long moment and then laughed nervously as they parted.

Fanny gathered up her long skirts in both

hands. "We're going to have to make a run for it," she warned. "Stay close."

He made sure she was protected by his coat. "Always, my lady. I am completely under your direction."

Chapter Twelve

Jeremy tightened his grip around Fanny's slender waist and hurried her the last few yards to Stapleton Manor through the hard downpour. They collapsed in the shelter of a stone archway but both of them were soaked through and unfit to be seen by anyone. "We'll have to get you out of those wet clothes."

"You're wet, too."

Jeremy's appearance hardly mattered in the greater scheme of things. Despite her wearing mourning black from head to toe, there were streaks of mud on Lady Rivers' skirts at the knees from where she'd slipped and fallen, taking Jeremy down with her. Her once-perfect gown had become a rag.

If they were seen so disheveled, people might imagine she'd been rutting with him in a field. With the contents of their contract known by Thwaite and Wilks, they might all too happily make baseless insinuations.

Jeremy couldn't allow that.

He had been at Stapleton long enough to have learned the most direct and discreet path to reach his chambers, and Fanny's chambers weren't too far along from there. He chivvied her up the first flight of stairs, checking at each turn for servants or a wandering guest.

At first their path was clear but when they reached the upper floor, they heard voices ahead of them. Jeremy pushed Fanny against a wall and held her there with his body. The Duke of Stapleton was talking with one of the servants not too far away.

Fanny stifled a laugh against his shoulder.

"Quiet," Jeremy warned, seeing nothing amusing in their predicament.

Fanny tried to peek past him, but he held her close and firmly away from the corner.

She wriggled against his body, standing on her tiptoes to loop her arms about his neck. Her breath was warm against his ear. "I haven't tried to sneak around behind my father's back since I was a girl," she whispered.

Her warm breath sent a thrill racing through every part of his body. Jeremy slowly glanced down into her upturned face. "You're lucky to have a father to sneak around behind," he murmured, fighting a shiver and something more.

He could see no sign that Fanny was alarmed by their proximity. In fact, she appeared to be cuddling up to him. She had, too, when he'd slept beside her, at odd times during the night. Right now, a droplet of rain was slowly sliding into her cleavage. Jeremy longed to lick that drop away, but not here in the hall where anyone might interrupt.

By God, Fanny was a woman to crave. Pretty

and used to getting what she wanted. He didn't mind that she'd thought he might share her bed one day, but he was surprised that she'd *want* him there, and a month ago it had been, too.

Her fingers stole into the hair at his nape and her lips parted on a sigh.

He eased away from temptation. "Your current state is entirely my fault."

"Yes, it is." A cheeky smile lifted the corners of her lips as her fingers spread over his chest. "What are you going to do about it?"

Jeremy scowled. She was daring him to misbehave, and right here where her father could find them. Here was further proof that this woman didn't play by society's rules. But he was trying to.

Jeremy peeked around the corner in time to see Stapleton turn into the stairwell and finally disappear. He waited a moment longer to be sure the duke was really gone and then grabbed Fanny by the hand to pull her out of hiding. He rushed her down the hall, and they reached her chambers without being seen. She produced a key and let herself in.

Jeremy followed and looked around. "Where's is that bloody maid of yours?"

Fanny chuckled. "My maid is never in my room at this time of day. I've no idea where she is, either, or desire to know. I like my privacy."

He shook his head. "You allow your maid, all your servants, to run roughshod over you."

Fanny shrugged and moved toward the far

windows to look outside and then turned to face him, her eyes alight. "The storm hasn't abated. It could be like this for hours…and no one will come to disturb us."

"I'll ring for your maid," he decided.

"Oh no, you won't." Fanny rushed to get between him and the bell. "All I need is a little help from you again."

Jeremy froze briefly then shook his head. Last time, he'd undressed her in the dark. He shouldn't undress Fanny in the daylight. Not with Thwaite and Wilks lurking about. "The maid would do a better job."

"Of undressing me?"

"Yes."

She popped a button undone at the front of her gown. "Of rinsing my skin clean and drying me?"

Jeremy gulped. Fanny was pushing his limits on purpose. "Yes, of course, the maid will be needed for that."

Fanny sidled closer, her face upturned to his. There was a streak of mud on her jaw, and more water droplets splattered on her now heaving chest from her dripping hair. *By God!* Even bedraggled she was stunning.

Jeremy trembled as she lay her hands upon his chest again.

"Fanny," he warned.

"There's no need to fight this."

"I must. One of us should give a damn about your reputation."

Fanny cupped his cheek. "You did me a great service retrieving my property from Wilks."

He pulled away immediately. "You'll not thank me like this."

Her gaze followed him. "Don't you find me attractive?"

He scowled at her. "You know I do."

Her attention dropped to his lips. "Please won't you kiss me, Jeremy? Please."

It was the second please that frayed his restraint. "Lady Rivers should never beg for attention."

"Then give me the kiss I've been waiting for."

Jeremy fought with his desires. He had wanted Lady Rivers since the moment they'd met. But that was in London, where casual flirtations were part and parcel with his profession. This was quite something else happening between them. They were playing with fire. She wanted to explore all the possibilities of their agreement. If he failed to please her, would she deny him her aid for everything else in the future? He wished with all his heart that he had never signed that damned agreement tant. "I should have no right to touch a woman like you."

She put her hands on her hips. "I'm only a woman."

"Lady Rivers, that does not even begin to describe you. This conversation is over." He turned his back on her, intending to go find a maid to help her change.

"Should I let Lord Wilks into my bed if he wants that, as well as paying his blackmail?"

Jeremy spun around to face her. "I have no right to deny you any pleasure."

"And yet when I tell you what I want, you refuse to even consider the notion."

"For God's sake. Do you not understand?"

Her eyes narrowed. "Then explain it. Use small words that my feeble female brain can accept."

He advanced on her, one finger raised. "Don't you ever talk about yourself like that again."

She shrugged, and the black rag she wore slipped to reveal dark undergarments. "Every other man since Rivers died has. They see the money and have to have me. They don't even try to know me first."

Jeremy took a pace toward her. "Fools."

"If you leave me, that's my only other choice. Fortune hunters and fools."

Jeremy growled. "That isn't a choice."

"But this is," she promised. "You are the man I crave above all others. You are the man I want to share my bed with."

Jeremy broke then, capturing Fanny by the head and jerked her into his arms. "Who needs a damn bed."

He crushed his lips to hers and stole the kiss he'd been dreaming of.

Fanny was soft and giving and so, so sweet.

Her arms stole around him, and Jeremy shivered at the contact. They were both still damp from the rain and there was probably a puddle forming beneath them that would be hard to explain later. Still he kissed her and wanted her and knew he wouldn't stop.

When she started pulling at his cravat, Jeremy wasted no time in stripping Fanny of her wet gown. Then he wrapped her in a blanket he stole from the bed and went on kissing her. When he started to struggle out of his own damp clothes, Fanny helped speed the process of his undressing.

"Oh, dear God," Fanny whispered when she stepped back as his breaches dropped to his knees after being undone. "What delights have I missed by putting proper clothes on you. Jeremy, you take my breath away."

Jeremy had to smile at that. Unlike the titled lords staying as the Duke of Stapleton's guests for the wedding, those who circled Fanny like vultures after her fortune, there was no comparison when it came to physicality. He was hard-muscled and sleek, a product of barely making ends meet all his life.

Fanny ran her hands all over his chest, teasing him without meaning to as the blanket fell from her shoulders and left her almost naked again. She flicked her fingers over his nipples, and then her lips were upon his skin. She licked him the way he'd wanted to lick her.

Reverently. Slowly. Seductively.

He grasped her by the hair and pulled her face up to his. "Fanny."

"Don't you like it?'

"You know I do."

He backed her toward the fire even as she shivered from the cold and undid the laces on her corset with some difficulty. He wanted to see her. All of her, before things went any further.

But once naked, Fanny huddled close and rubbed herself against him like a cat. Her breasts, works of art in his opinion, tortured as they dragged over his skin. He bent and took the nipple of one into his mouth. Fanny moaned and clutched his head to her breast. He rained kisses over her breasts and between.

"You make me feel weak, Jem," she whispered.

He couldn't have her falling into a swoon, so he put a hand across her buttocks and lowered her to her side on the thick Persian rug beneath them, keeping her close to the fire.

Fanny's arms encircled him again, and she found her way to his lips to kiss him. They lay before the fire, plastered together, tongues tangling and hands searching. Her body soft against his harder one as their kisses grew wilder, more passionate.

Jeremy pushed her damp hair from her face and stared into her eyes for a moment. "Are you sure you want *me*?"

"Never more so." To prove her words true, she

slung her leg over his hip, wriggling close enough that his cock brushed her curls.

Jeremy shuddered. He stole a kiss, and then another, and finally began to explore Fanny's thighs. She was warm and soft there, and he danced his rough fingertips along her limbs, then up to her hip and down again along her outer thigh. As he traced a return journey, he detoured inward, where her skin was most sensitive. He'd lain with women before, but he'd never had a proper lady want him, or touched any woman so thoroughly without clothing getting in the way. The excitement of her nakedness went completely to his head. His cock twitched, ached to be part of her.

But he was afraid to make a mistake. A woman of Fanny's class and experience, a widow of a satisfying and passionate marriage, had knowledge that far eclipsed his few paltry tumbles.

He hadn't the first idea of how to make love to her.

He kissed Fanny to hide his uncertainty as he fumbled about with his fingers against her curls.

Fanny enjoyed the kiss, but she suddenly gripped his wrist and held his hand still. Reluctantly, Jeremy drew back to look at her.

Her smile was shy. "May I show you what I like?"

He nodded quickly, embarrassed that his inexperience was so apparent.

Fanny captured a pillow from the settee and

put it under her head, then she slid her hand between her legs again. She traced the folds of her sex with her fingertips, drawing them through the dampest of places and up to the top of her slit.

Jeremy moved to rest his weight on one hand, hoping for a better view of what she was doing to herself.

"I don't mind if you watch," she whispered. "In fact, I find that exciting. Move closer."

Armed with permission, Jeremy wriggled down until his face was level with her quim. Fanny had a thatch of tight dark curls between her legs, and the skin of her slit was an alluring shade of pink.

Her fingers parted her folds and one digit brushed over a peak in the midst of her slit. "There. That is my clitoris. It is very sensitive and must be gently teased. A woman craves gentleness in this place in the beginning and can find great pleasure if it is touched or kissed by her lover." Fanny sighed and put her arm over her eyes. "I would enjoy you continuing to tease me like that, Jeremy."

He hardly needed the encouragement. He dragged his fingertips softly through Fanny's slit and then returned to the hard nubbin he'd quickly discovered made her moan. Fanny arched her hips up from the floor as he circled and stoked over that sensitive spot again and again. He thought he was doing the right thing, and Fanny's sighs and moans seemed to indicate he pleased her.

And then he remembered what she'd said about kissing her down there, too.

He moved closer and quickly pressed a kiss to her curls.

Fanny gasped. "Yes."

He did it again, exploring her slit with the tip of his tongue, his lips. Kissing her down there seemed to please her very much, so he moved between her thighs and continued. Fanny widened her legs, tilted her hips up to push her quim closer to his mouth.

He found the salty tang of her appealing and worked hard to drive her wild.

Fanny was nearly sobbing when she finally found her peak. She cried out and collapsed, appearing suddenly boneless as she let out a sigh.

Jeremy nuzzled her sex, feeling quite proud of himself for satisfying her. "I could do that all day if you wanted."

Fanny pushed his head away from her sex and closed her legs. "I am too sensitive for more."

"Oh," Jeremy said, disappointed to have to stop.

He sat back on his heels, uncertain if that was all she wanted from him. He was hard still. He ached for a completion of his own.

Fanny stirred, her legs parting slightly, then she raised her head to meet his gaze. "That was lovely. Come here, Jem."

He was perched over her in an instant.

Fanny ran her hands down his sides. Her

fingers gripped his hips and then skimmed his stomach to capture his cock in her hand. She stroked him slowly, making him moan.

She chuckled and her hands left his cock to squeeze the cheeks of his bottom. "When you are ready, I am too," she whispered.

Jeremy lowered his hips until his cock was nestled at the apex of her thighs, brushing moisture and heat. He almost groaned with anticipation of thrusting into her and finding his own release. But what if she didn't like the way Jeremy loved women? What if she was used to something different than he knew?

Fanny drew his head down to hers. "Jeremy, stop thinking."

"But—"

"I'm just like every other woman." She wriggled, and the head of his cock was notched just inside her body. "I want you now," she whispered and then caught his ear in her teeth.

Jeremy surged the rest of the way inside her, unable to stop himself. He pumped his hips, finding a rhythm quickly, watching her face for signs of disappointment.

Fanny's fingers tightened on him. She closed her eyes and made all the expected sounds of encouragement he needed. He was doing it right for her.

Jeremy braced himself on one arm above her, staring at her face. A delicate flush was climbing her cheeks. He nuzzled her there. "Fanny?"

"So good," she whispered.

"You are," he whispered back, then rose up on his hands.

Fanny's breasts jiggled along with his thrusts, and she suddenly cupped them. At first, he feared she was hiding them from him, but he soon realized she was playing with them, teasing her own nipples.

"Look at me," he demanded. She had to know it was him giving her this pleasure today and not herself.

Fanny opened her eyes slowly and continued to tug on her own nipples. "They like to be touched."

He lowered his mouth to kiss one when she offered it to him. A quick suck made her gasp, and her legs were suddenly wrapped higher around his waist, her body clinging to his where they joined. With only her shoulders and head upon the rug, he feared she would tire of the position, but she simply ran her hands down her body, toyed with his cock as it slipped in and out of her depths.

"I could have you like this all afternoon," he promised.

"I'll come again soon," she warned as her fingers were suddenly on her clit again.

Jeremy watched Fanny pleasure herself with her own fingers while his was cock buried inside her. It excited him to see her take charge of her own pleasure. "*Devil take it!*" he whispered in awe, twisting to see.

"I've a fierce need to feel you move inside me,"

she told him. "Give me everything you are and more."

Jeremy thrust, taking her hard until he thought his heart might burst from the pleasure of doing as he pleased. When Fanny suddenly squeezed around him and let out a muffled sob, coming around his cock, Jeremy gritted his teeth to hold back his own release. When he was confident, she'd wrung every moment of pleasure from the moment, he quickly withdrew, wrapped his hand around his cock and finished himself off.

Seed spilled over his fist, endangering the purity of the fine rug beneath them. He had to use both hands to capture it all, he was so excited. He knelt there a moment, trying to catch his breath with his eyes nearly squeezed shut to block out the delicious woman in front of him.

Fanny was suddenly on her hands and knees, coming close, and then her tongue flicked over the head of his cock. He felt her tongue glide around it. His cock gave another enthusiastic twitch and then he was engulfed in warmth. Jeremy opened his eyes fully to watch her have her wicked way with him.

Fanny finally sat back with a smirk gracing her lips. "I like the way you taste."

Despite its recent exertions, his cock twitched at the idea she might want to take him into her mouth again. "I always thought proper ladies were above that sort of thing."

"You'd be surprised. Some of us are quite experimental."

He frowned. "Have I not provided enough satisfaction?"

Fanny pulled him to her for a deep kiss. "I'd be happy to discuss all the forms of pleasure we might share when we have more time to indulge, Jeremy. As it is, I must go." Fanny rolled to her knees and then stood. "Would you help me dress? I have a blackmailer to meet and put in his place."

"Blackmailer?"

"Yes, Lord Thwaite insisted I meet with his son today to return the contract. No doubt he'll try to spring some sort of demand for money upon me then."

"You never said you were being blackmailed by Thwaite or his son."

She shrugged. "I never thought it was important to tell you."

"*I* consider it important, my lady."

"Why?" she shrugged again. "It will not be you paying their demands, not that I intend to give them one undeserving penny."

Jeremy put his hands on her shoulders to still her. "You already have the document in your safe. Why bother going?"

Fanny looked up at him. "I am a woman of my word, sir. I agreed to meet, and I will hear what Wilks has to say. And then I will refuse him. As you said earlier, they can do nothing without proof in their hands." Fanny moved away to sit before her dressing mirror, naked and lovely, but she grimaced. "Oh dear, there's the hoyden I used to be so long ago."

Jeremy moved to stand behind her, seeing nothing he'd change, but still concerned. "Hardly that."

"I look like I just tumbled down a steep slope. Several times."

Jeremy wet his lips. "About this meeting. I'm coming with you."

"No, you will not," she said firmly.

"Why not? I'm involved."

Fanny studied him in the mirror. "If you are there, it will only add fuel to their suspicions. But more importantly, I don't need a man to fight my battles for me."

"You needed me this week," he reminded her.

Her face softened a touch. "And I appreciate your friendship during this difficult time. I really do. And today was lovely, but sir, you have no right to involve yourself in my affairs just because we made love."

Jeremy flinched.

And Fanny was on her feet and before him in a second. "Now do not take offense. I need to do this alone. We'll get along better if you stop questioning every little thing I decide, sir. I wish I didn't have to go but I must."

Jeremy did not like this at all but what could he really do? If she didn't want him there, she didn't. That didn't mean he couldn't be of help. "Wilks is not to be trusted."

"Yes, I know that."

"You shouldn't be alone with him."

Fanny frowned. "I hardly require a chaperone."

"Don't argue. I'll not leave you alone with him."

She smiled. "I had no idea you were such a worrier."

Jeremy jerked his trousers on and tucked in his shirt, even though they were damp still. He'd have to change before he could follow her downstairs.

"Jeremy, have you ever laced a corset?"

"Once or twice. Why?"

"I'm going to need your help dressing." She studied him through narrowed eyes. "Whose corset did you lace?"

He laughed that she sounded jealous. He was also slightly baffled that she would be. "That would be my business."

Fanny's eyes narrowed even more, clearly unhappy that he didn't provide her with an answer. That was just too bad. If she wanted to keep him at arm's length, he would do the same. She couldn't have everything her way.

He snatched up her damp corset, but she handed him another dry one instead. "Don't lace me so tight that I cannot breathe. I need breath to give Wilks a piece of my mind."

"As you wish, my lady," he replied with a short bow that he hoped would irritate her.

Chapter Thirteen

Lord Wilks sauntered into their meeting twenty minutes later than Fanny had expected him to arrive. She was annoyed with him, and with the conversation she'd just had with Jeremy. The way they'd parted had left a bad taste in her mouth. One coupling did not make him privy to all of her business, even if making love to him had been better than she'd ever dreamed.

"My dear Lady Rivers, do forgive my tardy arrival," Wilks drawled.

She would not. She would secretly hold that against him for years to come. She was a busy woman who knew her own mind and held private grudges. Fanny regarded him standing in the doorway, her jaw clenching momentarily before relaxing. The sooner this farce of a meeting was over and done with the better. She looked Wilks over but did not see any papers in his hands. "Lord Wilks."

He glanced around the room, one brow arching. It was just the two of them. Fanny had not wanted any witnesses to her embarrassment. Especially not Jeremy, though she was touched by his concern. "I'm so glad you could see me. *Alone* too," he drawled again.

Fanny regarded him warily now. "What is it that you want?"

"We'll get to that."

She glanced across to the empty chair opposite. "Please, won't you sit."

He made a circuit of the room and then swooped to sit close beside her. "Where is your cicisbeo today?"

Fanny didn't bother to answer that. A cicisbeo waited on *married* women. Fanny was a widow, engaged in an affair. There was nothing wrong with her arrangement with Jeremy. Nothing at all when she betrayed no one. And what she did with Jeremy was no one's business. "Your father promised the return of an important document of mine if I met with you today."

Wilks smirked. "My father makes a lot of promises to me, too. Few of which I think he'll honor unless I do as he wishes. He wished us to get to know each other better," Wilks said with a smirk.

Fanny gritted her teeth. Clearly, Wilks planned to go along with that. He would also make her wait or beg for the document's return. Jeremy insisted she should never beg. "I'm afraid your father will be doomed to disappointment, my lord. So will you."

"I think not," Wilks promised, turning toward her. "As I'm sure you've heard, my father's tight fist has presented unacceptable difficulties for the running of Holly Field."

"Your Devon estate? Yes, I've heard you've been living well beyond your means."

Wilks glared at her. "Lies," he hissed. "My father doles just enough blunt to keep me in line until the next quarter day. I haven't had the funds to make improvements in years."

Fanny doubted that. She'd seen Wilks gamble recklessly with her own eyes. "I still fail to see how this is any of my concern."

"You could help me get out from under my father's thumb," Wilks murmured. "I'd make a good husband."

Fanny laughed. "Is that right?"

He shuffled closer along the bench until his knee brushed hers.

Fanny barely stopped herself from launching herself out of her chair. She kept her hands folded in her lap though, ready to punch him in the nose if he had plans to force a match between them. "I've made no secret of my disinterest in remarriage."

"You'll change your tune when society turns its back on you." He smirked. "You'll find marriage to me the better alternative to the cold of a thousand cuts."

Fanny had been on the outs with society before. Over Gillian, actually, but clearly Wilks thought her weak and malleable. "What could possibly cause such an event?"

"If a certain document with your signature upon it fell into the wrong hands, well…"

He left the threat unfinished.

Fanny had had enough. She had his measure now. He wanted *all* her money, not just a token amount. She loathed men like him, and his father, too. "Do you refer to the document you have right there in your pocket? The document you intend to blackmail me with to ensure we marry so you can fritter away my fortune on wine, other women and cards?"

He smiled as if she was finally catching on.

"You might have been moderately convincing if I didn't have that document safely locked away already, my lord."

Wilks froze, eyes boring into hers.

Fanny stood and went to ring the bell. "Since you have nothing truly important to say to me or give back, I believe we have nothing further to say to each other."

Wilks was on his feet and rushing her, crowding her until she stumbled back. "I still know what it says," he hissed.

"Do you believe everyone is always eager to believe fabrications? That hasn't been my experience with society," she warned.

Wilks drew back. "Anyone can see Dawes is in love with you."

Fanny's heart gave an odd lurch. "He is an actor. A very good one. That's why he won my patronage over an actor with years more experience. He's fooled you into thinking he was in love with me because I asked him to play a part.

Father approved our little play and has been coaching him on the habits of society gentlemen. He has learned a lot this past week."

A momentary expression of doubt flickered over Wilks' face but he drew back even further. "So, you're not involved with the actor."

"He's an amusing companion and plays no part in my decisions."

A door opened and Fenton, steward of the Stapleton estate, stomped into the room looking unusually cross. Also, as usual, he carried a stout stick that he tapped on the floor as he walked toward her. "Dawes ordered me to come see you, Lady Rivers."

As happy as she was to have Fenton in the room her heart sank as Wilks smirked. "Orders the servants about already, does he. I rather think there's more to his position in your life than you want to admit, my lady. How far the mighty have fallen. Paying a man to make love to you and falling for him, too."

Fanny ground her teeth. *Jeremy!*

Why couldn't he have trusted her to take care of the matter without him. He had no right to interfere in her business. She couldn't have been clearer. She had almost had Wilks convinced there was no gain to be had gossiping about a contract he didn't have a copy of. "The only thing I have almost fallen for were your lies, and your father's. Fenton, Lord Wilks has expressed a desire to leave the estate. Do be so kind as to have his luggage brought down so he might depart immediately."

Fenton twirled his stick menacingly. "A pleasure, my lady. Oh, and his grace wishes to see you when you are free."

"I am free now in fact," she promised, glancing at Wilks without smiling. "Goodbye, my lord."

Wilks wet his lips. "This isn't over. My father will—"

"Yes, I'm sure he will try anything to get what he wants," Fanny murmured. "Do make sure to remind your father that I *was* still considering the opportunity he was so anxious to have me invest in. His actions will guide my final decision."

"When you are ready, my lord," Fenton murmured, stepping closer to Wilks with a hard thump of his stick upon the floor.

Wilks looked ready to argue but then strode off when Fenton swung his stick again.

"His grace is waiting in the library," Fenton said to Fanny grinning before he slipped from the chamber, following Wilks.

When they couldn't be heard anymore, Fanny swore and then left the chamber to report to her father in the library.

Father beamed when he saw her, rising from a chair by the fire. "Ah, Fanny. There you are at last."

"Were you looking for me for very long, Papa?"

"It's always too long." Father crossed the room to meet her and pressed a kiss to her brow.

"Come in and talk to your poor old father. You're looking a little flushed. Has something upset you?"

"No." On an impulse, Fanny wrapped her arms around her papa and gave him a squeeze. He was one of the good ones, and good men were so very rare. He hugged her back, then set her apart from him. "What was that for?"

"I just needed it."

He made a grumbling sound, but she could tell he was pleased. "Come and sit down with me."

She made a point of looking around carefully. "Are you sure you want a woman in the library? I thought that was against the rules."

He gave her a look. "Are you going to suggest putting flowers in this room?"

"No."

"Lacy doily things on the tables?"

She smiled. "No. I know you hate them."

"Then you can stay, but if you dare mention the room needs improvement, you'll be out the door before you can blink, and I'll never speak to you again."

Fanny laughed. Father had changed too when he'd married Gillian. He was finally mellowing about his rules. "It won't work, Father. You're too tenderhearted to stay cross with any of us girls forever."

He huffed.

"I'd never want to be at odds with you about anything anyway."

His brow rose. "Tell me how you're doing, my girl. Are you as happy as you seem?"

Fanny breathed a sigh of relief. Father didn't know about Thwaite, Wilks or any blackmail. Jeremy had kept his world to let her at least handle that alone. She was thankful beyond measure for that. "I am happy," she promised.

Father smiled. "Vastly content I would say, judging by that smile."

"I suppose so," she murmured, feeling not the least bit guilty. She had more or less dealt with Wilks who was a spineless worm in her opinion. The father was another matter. She would deal with Thwaite one day soon—in a way he'd never suspect her for, too.

"It had to happen eventually."

"What do you mean?"

"All that money you inherited has worried me, for it only added to your burdens."

She smiled. "I thrive on challenges."

"I've always worried you'd work yourself to death to build your late husband's fortunes, but no more. I've seen a side of you, on this visit particularly, that pleases me no end."

"Weddings make for happiness. I am so pleased for Rebecca and Jessica, and you too, of course."

"I am not talking about your sisters and I, but of you. You have made a change in your life recently that has only been beneficial, as far as I can tell."

"What change would that be?"

"Mr. Jeremy Dawes."

Fanny met his gaze…and saw a scold hovering in his expression now.

He inclined his head. "I'm not blind."

"I never imagined you were."

Father shook his head. "You've been discreet, I'll give you that, but I know full well what goes on in my own house."

"He has played his part very well," she said. "There is nothing going on between us, I assure you."

"Now that is a lie." Father frowned. "Did I say I disapprove?"

Fanny blinked. "No but… Wealthy men take lovers all the time and no one bats an eye. I just assumed you would, too."

"Most women do not take so many risks with their reputations. Women are expected to marry and live respectably."

She shook her head. "I'll not adhere to society's rules and restrictions and suddenly become biddable just because we slept together."

"So, he *has* shared your bed then?"

Fanny closed her eyes, annoyed that she'd fallen for Father's little trick and revealed the truth of her association with Jeremy. He'd made a guess, a correct one, and she'd confirmed it. She'd thought she'd grown out of that sort of thing long ago.

But Father looked pleased with himself. "Can't

wriggle out of that confession, my girl. A few nights, I would you say."

"Yes."

"Of course, you know there'd be gossip about him," Father warned. "He's no connections or real wealth. You risk losing the respect of your peers. Marriage would of course make any scandal disappear."

Fanny was shocked by her father's suggestion. "I am certainly not going to marry to avoid a scandal."

"Of course you shouldn't when you have the choice of marrying for love instead. Imagine if he presented himself to his theater manager once word spreads, I bet he would land a starring role. Imagine the crowd he'd draw. The man who had tamed Lady Fanny Rivers. He'd be a valuable commodity."

"He would not seek to benefit in that way," she insisted.

Father seemed surprised by her response. "Why shouldn't he earn his way in the world? Or have you paid him so well for his company that he might never need to perform again?"

"The sum I have given him is fair," she promised. "But it might be wise to revise the terms of their arrangement to ensure he wouldn't seek to profit from a scandal.

"There's more to him than meets the eye then, as you claimed from the beginning." He shrugged. "Secret affairs do not last forever, and it is my fervent hope that Dawes will not cause a fuss."

The idea of that happening sent a shiver down Fanny's spine, but she gritted her teeth to hide her fear. Jeremy's *role* in her life was fleeting. Father's warning was timely for her not to forget that. Not to be swept away by her growing infatuation. She had no future with Jeremy. They were acting the part of friends and lovers. "Have you seen him this afternoon?"

"I saw him talking with Wilks earlier," Father said in an offhand way. "I'm sure he'll come back. He usually does."

"Yes," Fanny agreed, starting to climb to her feet.

Father smiled. "Well, I'd best go find my Gillian."

"Yes of course. Give her my love."

"I will."

Father sauntered out ahead of her.

Fanny waited a beat then hurried upstairs, looking for Jeremy. She went first to her own chamber, finding it still locked, and then went to her safe. She'd made a careful study of Jeremy unlocking her safe, and she'd learned the trick of opening it up herself very quickly.

Once she had what she required, she slipped along to the guest bedroom Jeremy had been given and tapped on his door, then let herself in.

Jeremy appeared caught by surprise, quickly shoving whatever he'd been reading behind him.

Fanny narrowed her eyes. "What are you doing?"

"Nothing important."

"Show me what's behind your back."

His cheeks turned red as he reluctantly produced a slim volume. Fanny snatched it up to read the cover.

It was a book for children, surely not his, but a well-read one taken from the family library downstairs. She handed it back. "Are you not a bit old for nursery tales?"

Jeremy grimaced. "What did you want to see me for?"

For so much that she almost for a moment doubted her decision. But it was the right thing to do to protect her reputation. He could stay in her life but he would advance his career because of his own hard work. She'd always doubt his affections otherwise and that would grow and spoil any friendship between them. "I want to honor your work."

A frown creased his face, and he stood. "Why?"

"While my initial idea was a good one, unfortunately, your performance was a little too convincing for certain people." She waved her hand about in the direction of his bed. "And what happened between us, while enjoyable, should not happen again."

He folded his arms over his chest. "So just like that, you're done with me."

"Now, Mr. Dawes, we both knew it was a risk I

was taking with my reputation pretending you were my beau. Wilks has gone, Thwaite too. Letterford has set his sights on another. All the guests are departing today. From now on, I prefer a clear distinction between your performance here and the reality of our relationship."

She waved their agreement in the air and committed it to the flames. "Good riddance. I'll write another upon my return to London. One with better terms to see you rise through the ranks of the theatre."

"I don't need another agreement."

"We both know your heart's desire is to perform before an adoring audience in London," she chided. She produced a wad of money from her reticule and held it out.

He looked at it with suspicion. "What's that?"

"Your bonus for an outstanding performance here," she told him. "You can count it if you like but I promise I'd never short-change anyone so talented."

"Thank you, but no." Jeremy turned away and started gathering up his possessions.

Fanny looked at her hand full of money, then at him. "What are you doing? Was it not enough?"

"I don't deserve a single penny. I thought … I thought I had earned your respect, but it's clear to see I don't have any such thing if at the first argument between us has you throwing your money around."

"I could pay you more if I must?"

"I don't want more. I don't want any." He riffled through the closet but removed nothing before he shut the door. "I'll leave all of this lot for your next stray, shall I? It shouldn't be too hard to find a man of my build if you frequent the poorer parts of London. We're all underfed and grateful for a rich lady's charity."

"My next? Sir, you go too far!"

"Too far with *you*. Everyone told me you're fond of taking in strays. Perfumed imbeciles. Where are they now? Well-funded by your charity still. I'm nothing like those men." He looked at her a long time, a look of hopelessness coming into his eyes she'd never seen there before. He brushed past her on the way to the door.

"Jeremy." Fanny rushed after him. "Where do you think you are going?"

"What do you care?"

"I never said I didn't care about you!"

He was suddenly towering over her. "You offered me that money because I shared your bed, admit it, not because of my *performance* in front of your friends and family."

She grabbed hold of his arm. "Quiet. Someone in the hall might hear you."

"What does it matter? I'll be gone and forgotten in a moment anyway."

She blanched. "Jeremy, calm down. Let's talk about this."

He perched a shabby wool cap on his head and pulled it low over his eyes. "It's Mr. Dawes to you from now on, Lady Rivers. I've got my own code of honor, and the first item is to never fuck someone who wants to pay me for the privilege."

"Jere—Mr. Dawes, please. There's no need for you to be upset and leave in a huff. I am only living up to my promise to you."

"A huff? Madam, I am deeply insulted."

Fanny gaped. "What is so wrong with me doing the right thing by you? You need the money, don't you?"

"Not as much as you must imagine." Then, after taking one last look around, he snatched up a canvas sack and marched out the door without meeting her gaze again.

Chapter Fourteen

Never again would Jeremy accept the patronage of a wealthy widow, unless she was a wizened old crone with no teeth. Just when he'd thought he had earned Fanny's respect, he learned he'd never had it at all.

Jeremy marched toward the front door, full of righteous rage and disgust with her offer of money. How dare Fanny belittle his friendship, their connection, by offering to pay him more money just because he'd slept with her. He'd gone to her bed because he'd wanted *her*, not her money. Just her. The woman who he'd thought wanted him, too.

Apparently, he'd gravely mistaken the nature of her interest.

He was just a cock and a pair of willing lips to her. A pretend friend, a discardable commodity.

"Mr. Dawes! Just the man I want to see," the Duke of Stapleton called out as he passed the entrance to the library.

Jeremy came to a complete halt inches away from escape and cursed under his breath. If it had been any other man, he would have ignored him. Jeremy pivoted slowly, finding the Duke of

Stapleton emerging from the shadows of the chamber, as he'd done on the first day of his arrival at Stapleton Manor. He was even dressed the same. How had Jeremy mistaken his identity?

The duke looked him up and down, a frown growing on his face. "Going somewhere?"

Jeremy clutched his sack of few precious possessions under his arm. There was no point in pretending he wasn't attempting to slip away. "Yes. Back to London. Like everyone else."

The duke took a slow step in his direction. "To do what?"

"Return to the theater, I suppose."

"Ah," the duke murmured. "That *is* a surprise."

"It shouldn't be," Jeremy said, glancing toward the door. Just a few more steps and freedom would be his. "You should be glad to see the back of me, I imagine."

"You imagine wrong." The duke gestured toward the library behind him. "Might we speak a moment before you go?"

Jeremy had grown to like and respect the duke and had time to spare, now the arrangement with the duke's daughter had ended. Besides, the duke had housed him for the past week, largely without complaint. He could spare him a little time. "Of course."

"Good. Come this way," Stapleton ordered.

Once Jeremy was past the archway, the duke shut and locked the door behind them. That amused Jeremy so much, he grinned. There wasn't a lock he couldn't pick. This house, and all its treasures, could have been his if he'd wanted to remain a thief instead of trying to live as an honest man. "What did you want to talk to me about?"

"Do sit down." The duke settled into a chair, appearing relaxed, and gestured for Jeremy to do the same. "Tell me what you remember of your parents."

The duke had asked that question before, and Jeremy shrugged at his dogged hunt for information about him. "I really don't know anything about them. They died when I was young."

"Do you know where you were born and when?"

Jeremy tensed. "London. Somewhere in the city. Don't know the date."

The duke's brows shot up. "You don't know your exact age?"

"No. I've always assumed I was about three when they passed."

The duke nodded, clearly mulling over that fact. "If your parents died so long ago that you cannot remember them, who raised you?"

Jeremy did not want to answer questions. He would rather forget there was no one in the world who cared about him. He moved to stand behind his chair, facing the duke. "I'm sorry I don't have answers to the questions you're asking."

"I am, too. The past influences any chance of

success in any future, as I'm sure you're already aware."

Jeremy glanced toward the door, knowing he should be on his way if he had any hope of catching the afternoon mail coach returning to London.

"I know you can pick that lock, son, and you are free to leave at any time you choose," Stapleton promised in a low voice. "The door is locked to keep everyone else out while we talk about your future."

Jeremy froze a moment, then whipped his head around to face the duke.

"If you won't take the time to explain yourself, a father must do his own investigating." The man smiled. "I know any discussion of your past is a discomfort to you and likely for very good reasons. I cannot begin to imagine what you must have endured. But if I am to help you, then I insist on full disclosure here and now. I cannot protect my family if I don't know what might one day become a threat."

Jeremy clenched the back of the chair. "I'm no threat to your family."

"I believe you, and I *am* glad. Glad for you, and for my daughter, too."

"She doesn't need to know anything else about me. Not now."

"Fanny probably suspects a lot more than she lets on." The duke smiled. "Raised among thieves, you've come a long way from Seven Dials."

The hair on the back of Jeremy's neck rose. "I never said that I—"

"Didn't have to. You don't get to be my age without developing the skill of reading between the lines. As I mentioned when we first met, my daughter is fond of taking in strays. The more hopeless the case, the better. She has a knack of bringing out the best in most people she helps, though."

Jeremy scowled, angry at hearing yet again that he was a charity case. None of them would let him forget it. "Her so-called generosity will bring her nothing but trouble, you know."

"I think so too, which makes you the perfect man for the position I have in mind."

Jeremy frowned. "What position would that be?"

"As her husband."

"I never… I didn't."

The duke smiled. "There they are. The words of a man terrified a father might call him out for kissing his daughter."

Jeremy gulped.

"More than kissing?" The duke shook his head. "I don't need to know how far along your courtship has gone, only that it is a fact—and I expect you to marry my daughter, or I will make your life extremely uncomfortable."

Every muscle in Jeremy's body tightened, ready to take flight. "You can't be serious. You'd hitch her to a *gormless diver* just to spare her the shame of having everyone know I got under her skirts?"

"Gormless?" The duke stood abruptly and drew closer. "Never, *ever* let me hear you speak of yourself like that again. It is beneath you."

Jeremy drew back. "It's what I am. A thief. She thinks I'm no better than a wh—" But he failed to complete that sentence. "I haven't a clue what she wants but it will never be me."

"Let me give you a little bit of advice since you seem dense to certain facts: there are no men in this world who can provide a woman with *everything* they wants."

"Then why would you want her wed?"

"Because I'm growing older, son. I know what it's like to not have someone, a best friend, by your side. To be overwhelmed by difficult choices and have no one you trust completely to confide in. I had my children, yes, but it is not the same as having a spouse." The duke caught his eye. "Do you realize my second wife was one of Fanny's strays?"

Jeremy shook his head quickly.

"Fanny rescued Gillian from a cruel employer. I won't go into the details now but suffice to say, Fanny fought a dragon to free her and won herself another firm friend. But she made an enemy in society, too. Fanny, in her usual reckless fashion, took my Gillian home to stay with her—promising to help her find a better position. I feared the worst, of course, given that many of Fanny's strays seem to hang about for far too long. But I found a use for Gillian as a paid companion to my youngest daughter."

"You married her."

"No one ever plans to fall in love. It just happens." The duke put his hands to Jeremy's shoulders and propelled him back to his former chair, pushing him down to sit in it. "I married Gillian after nearly a year of getting to know each other because our interest in each other was too strong to ignore. One of my daughters disapproved of Gillian strenuously and almost ruined my chances of winning her hand. But we eventually married, and we've been happily going along together ever since." The duke smiled. "My point is, no matter the difficulties, they can be overcome very easily—but only if you talk through them."

Jeremy squinted at the duke. The man clearly didn't know *what* he was talking about. "She wanted to pay me for sleeping with her."

The duke winced. "Badly done, and a sign that I was right. My daughter needs you."

"She doesn't need anything money can't buy," Jeremy said, feeling bitterness rise up inside him again.

The duke held up one hand, fingers spread, and ticked off each finger as he spoke. "Respect. Understanding. Patience. Protection on occasion. Eternal admiration. Did I mention patience? The fact that she tried to place limits on your relationship speaks volumes. She has considered where you might fit in her life."

Jeremy shook his head. "She doesn't want me."

"She does, and even now, you're having doubts about leaving, too, I can tell." The duke pointed at him. "You respect my daughter—her intelligence, her capability. You also understand the many dangers that she'll face in the coming years better than anyone. The more wealth she accumulates, the more the needy will flock to her door. Her heart will be touched again and again as she gives whatever is asked of her to the undeserving."

"She is too generous with her charity," Jeremy murmured. "She'll run out of money one day."

"A long time from now, I expect. Fanny does have considerable resources at her command," the duke mused.

Jeremy frowned. "If you say so."

The duke inhaled, studying him closely again. "You don't know what it means to have great wealth, do you? Not really. You've heard people talk, but you don't truly comprehend just how large a fortune she has at her command."

Jeremy shrugged. "I never had any real money until I met Fanny. I mean, Lady Rivers."

"No need to apologize." The duke sat forward. "Put the first coin that Fanny gave you on your palm."

Jeremy dug in his pocket for his lucky shilling. The coin he'd earned for escorting her to her carriage the day they'd met had felt important to keep…but not anymore.

The duke smiled. "I knew you'd still have it."

Jeremy squirmed again. Did it make him appear pathetic? "Do you want it back?"

"No, I want you to imagine many more, until your hand is completely covered."

Jeremy did. He'd be a wealthy man indeed if he had all that. "It's more than I could ever earn in my life."

The duke sat forward even more. "Now, I want you to look around the room and put piles of money on every surface. Then add more and more and more, until all the furniture is covered. Can you do that?"

"Yes. It's a king's ransom."

"Now imagine the room full to the ceiling. *That* is how much wealth my daughter has at her disposal, I suspect."

Jeremy gulped. "You suspect?"

"Well, Fanny doesn't have to confide in her poor old father when she's a great deal smarter than I am. But don't tell her I said that. She'd preen for days."

Jeremy shook her head. "She probably would, too."

"Wealthy and smart Fanny may be, but giving to others is not necessarily enough to satisfy her anymore. In short, she needs a family."

"She has a family." The Westfalls were a family unlike any he'd ever met. They were always sticking their noses into each other's concerns. They fought and made up and laughed and loved each other. It made Jeremy envious, to be honest. He'd never have that.

"And we all love her dearly, but I'll put this plainly. My daughter needs her own family. She needs someone to pass her extraordinary wealth and talents to one day. She needs a husband she can trust with her heart and fortune, who can lure her away from her ledgers and make her remember she has other interests. Someone who can steal her away to sit in the sunshine or stay in bed with her on a rainy day. A man who will let her return to her responsibilities without bitterness or resentment of her intelligence. In short, my daughter needs not a man to take over her fortune, but a partner for a more balanced life."

"There are many who would marry her. Someone of her class would do."

The duke waved his hand about as if brushing the suggestion away. "Son, the way you feel about my daughter, and overlook the importance of her money, is very rare. I've only ever known of one man before who didn't feel threatened by her fascination for business and finance."

"She should marry him," Jeremy suggested bitterly.

"Fanny did. The late Lord Rivers let her have her head in all matters that interested her, even when society dictated that such passions in women be repressed. Fanny made him a very rich man before he died. He adored every inch of her, body and mind, yet he couldn't give her children, and he died before his time."

Jeremy sat in silence a moment. "You've rocks in your head if you think we'd make a good match. How do you know she even wants children?"

"She didn't want dance lessons either until her sister took them." The duke confessed with a laugh. "I admit, on the surface, it seems a tad unequal an alliance."

"I'll say," Jeremy agreed.

"Money *is* the only obstacle," the duke countered. "And agreements can be drawn up to protect and limit your access to her funds, if need be."

It would be another document Jeremy wouldn't understand. "I'm illiterate."

"Something you've managed to conceal from her, I suspect." The duke sighed. "Fanny's fear is being desired for only her money. Yours is being known."

"That's ridiculous," Jeremy protested.

"Many men have courted her since she became a widow. From ambitious squire to aging duke, even a foreign prince dangled the hint of a crown in her direction once. Every single one proved themselves merely fortune hunters. Fanny doesn't have the best of luck when it comes to men. She's become distrustful and wary of forming attachments, which is why she attempted to pay you off, I imagine. But I won't let you slip away without fighting to make her see this is her chance to have everything she's ever secretly wanted and was too afraid to reach for."

Jeremy squinted at the duke. "What's in it for you?"

The duke smiled. "Grandbabies."

Jeremy rolled his eyes. The duke was soon to become a father again and yet still wanted more babies in the family? "You ask too much."

"There's something in the way my daughter has softened since you've been around. I thought our little talk earlier might have propelled her to see you in a new light," Stapleton admitted.

"She certainly did, but clearly not the way you'd intended." Jeremy shook his head and stood again. "It's all very well for you to sit here discussing a future that will never come to pass. I'm done, and I'm seeing myself out now. Goodbye, your grace."

The duke was on his feet and between Jeremy and the door before he realized his intent. "You can't leave."

"You can't stop me," Jeremy warned.

"If you return to the theater, what's the chance that you won't be reduced to dressing the principal actors again? You won't have Fanny's patronage to give them reason to cast you over someone with more experience. Fanny has loved the theater since she was a girl. You will see her again there, too."

Jeremy blanched. Seeing Fanny sitting above him in the audience, so close and yet so far, wouldn't be enjoyable. "If I don't land a part without her patronage, I'll find somewhere else to belong. Another company might take me on."

"Is it easy for you to find somewhere to belong?" the duke asked.

A sick feeling churned in his belly, but Jeremy was no stranger to having to work hard. "I'll do all right. Move."

"No."

Jeremy looked up at the duke. The man outranked him, and he outweighed him by several stone. Could probably box him into the floorboards, too. Jeremy didn't want to end up in a physical altercation with the duke if he could help it but his time here had come to an end. His best defense had always been slipping away unnoticed, but the duke wouldn't let him. "Please move."

Stapleton shook his head. "You will stay and see what happens with Fanny."

Jeremy squinted at the man. "Why are you *really* trying to keep me here?"

"I should have known you wouldn't be convinced by my talk of legacy." The duke chuckled. "All right, I want you to stay because I see something in you that I cannot ignore."

"What is that?"

"Potential, beyond that of a mere actor." The duke nodded. "Stay another week."

"I can't. It was Fanny who brought me here, and I swore to leave."

"All right then. Leave."

The duke suddenly unlocked the library door, caught Jeremy by the elbow, and dragged him out the huge front door. Although Jeremy tried to free himself, the duke had a surprisingly strong grip for an older man. He was also adamant Jeremy leave Stapleton with nothing more than the clothes on his back. Jeremy's satchel had been left forgotten on the floor of the library.

The wide-open lawn and long, empty drive stretched before him. Freedom. He was on his own again. He should feel better about that than he did.

The duke extended his hand. "Mr. Dawes, I'm glad to have met you."

"Thank you," Jeremy replied as he shook it. "Thank you for having me."

"My pleasure," the duke said, as he suddenly spun Jeremy about so he faced the front door to Stapleton Manor once more. The duke shook his hand repeatedly. "So good of you to visit again, Mr. Dawes. How was your journey? I'll have a servant prepare your *new* room in no time at all."

Jeremy tried to escape the duke's grip and couldn't. "But I'm leaving?"

"No. You *left*. But now you are being welcomed back to Stapleton Manor as the Duke of Stapleton's honored guest, not his daughter's." The duke laughed. "A simple solution, don't you think?"

Jeremy stared at the duke in awe. "Now that is really splitting hairs, your grace."

The duke ushered him back through the front door and past a footman before turning into the library again. "In private, you may address me as Nicolas."

"I couldn't do that," he whispered, still stunned.

"Marry Fanny, and I might even answer to Papa." Jeremy was forced down into another chair and the duke sat beside him. "So, you will stay at Stapleton as my guest, yes? For as long as it takes for Fanny to come to her senses and admit she made a ghastly mistake. By all means, make her suffer a bit if it makes you happy. Money brings rewards all too easily for those in our circles.

"And remind me, I must take you out shooting and riding. Given the future I wish for you, it would be best to take the time now to judge if you are adept at either sport or decide if lessons will be needed. Fanny will need you by her side at a great many society gatherings in the coming years. House parties and the season. Not to mention family celebrations. I will also send my valet to you each morning. He worked as a tutor in Leeds before we met. He will be of great help in improving your literacy."

Jeremy squinted at the duke. "He was a stray of yours, wasn't he?"

Stapleton threw his arms wide. "Fanny had to acquire her bad habits from someone."

Jeremy chewed his lip. "What if she isn't pleased to see me?"

"Son, leave my daughter be at first. Make her wonder and miss what she had. I've had years more experience in getting Fanny to do things she doesn't want to do than you." The duke rubbed his hands together. "But this is not just about her. Have you ever held a pistol?"

Jeremy shook his head. The duke was an odd fellow. But what was the harm in staying a few days more if there was a promise of receiving instruction? It wasn't as if Jeremy had anywhere pressing to be. If Fanny really didn't believe they had any future together, the duke could still help him learn to read and write, and that could only be to his advantage. He wasn't too proud to accept help. A tutor was an expense Jeremy would never be able to afford. And the other skills might come in handy one day, too.

Jeremy stood and strolled to a glass-faced cabinet that held a range of pistols and studied them. "I've never shot anything," he admitted. "I've been shot at, though."

The duke joined him and unlocked a cabinet to pass Jeremy a small pistol to look at. "We aim at the birds here, not at each other. Occasionally poachers. Tomorrow at dawn, we will see what sort of marksman you might become."

"I'll do my best."

The duke grinned. "I expect nothing less of you."

He glanced up at the duke. "I hope you don't live to regret this."

"My only regret would have been if Fanny had successfully driven you away."

"She still could," Jeremy warned. "I'm not exactly the man of her dreams, am I?"

The duke chuckled softly. "Son, I think you'll be pleasantly surprised."

Chapter Fifteen

Fanny did not like babies. Or rather, she did, but they often made her feel inadequate. She sat in the morning room beside Jessica and Rebecca, who were gushing over the Hawthorne's youngest babe who'd come to stay with the duchess as if the child was their own. It was an awkward place to be when she'd never be likely to have offspring herself.

"Were the Hawthorne women well when you last spoke to them?" Fanny asked, trying to draw her sister Jessica's attention away from the gurgling child.

"Destroyed and trying not to show it," Jessica murmured. "It is so hard to see their long faces and know there is nothing I can do to cheer them."

"Give them time. You have done your best, I'm sure," Fanny promised, declining to take the child from Rebecca when she tried to pass the wriggling infant to her.

Rebecca huffed and sat the babe back on her lap. "How can you not want to hold such a scrumptious morsel?"

"He is a babe, not food." Fanny forced a smile. Rebecca had become decidedly keen on children. Not surprising since she was increasing herself now too. "Clarice would never forgive me if I dropped him."

"You never dropped Jessica," she noted.

Fanny cast a quick glance at her sister and smiled. "That anyone saw," she teased.

Jessica gaped. "Did you?"

Fanny chuckled. "I was only pulling your leg, little one. It was Samuel who dropped you. Thankfully, you bounced very neatly on the mattress and came to no harm."

"Pay her no mind. He never dropped you. None of us did anything of the sort." Rebecca promised Jessica. "Father would have murdered us for being careless."

The baby moved to Jessica's arms and he cuddled up to her, making all sorts of happy sounds. "Don't worry little Liam," she promised. "I'll love you even if Aunt Fanny won't."

Fanny stood and moved to look out the window. They'd all suddenly become Aunts to the Hawthorne brood since the death. While she didn't mind the term of affection, it did make her feel old. "I can love him from a distance, too."

Jeremy had left yesterday. A bitter parting that made her uneasy today. She should be happy to be spared further argument over his place in her life. Clearly, he'd thought something else had happened between them than just sex.

It was for the best that he was gone. Now she could turn her attention to assessing the investment opportunity Lord Thwaite had been trying to interest her in. She was inclined to say no to him out of spite because of his attempted blackmail. But there were other investors involved and there was the rumor he couldn't now afford it. The project deserved a fair and unbiased final assessment before she turned her attention to her next project.

Unfortunately, she felt no keen desire for anything right now.

She turned to observe her sisters. They were happy, even though they all wore the black of mourning for their friend and neighbor. Ever since Father's wedding last year, the mood of the family had changed subtly. Where before they had all been unlucky in love, now one by one, her siblings were making happy matches, and babies as well. No wonder people remarked that she should be next. Fanny returned to her chair. "When will you go back to your husbands?"

"Today," Jessica promised. "I was on my way home now but wanted to see if you were still here."

"I've no plans to leave," Fanny promised. Besides, Jeremy would arrive in London most likely tomorrow, and she wanted to give him time to cool his temper before she saw him again.

If they met again.

She bit her lip. She has spent last night tossing and turning. There *was* a chance she might never see Jeremy if he didn't want to see her.

"You never do tell anyone," Jessica complained. "You're just suddenly gone."

Rebecca sighed. "Jessica, not now!"

"Now is the perfect time. We both think she's become as restless as Samuel. Always on the hunt for the next adventure, the next investment, that will make her richer but not happier."

"That is enough, sister," Rebecca warned, eyes flashing disapproval for Jessica's rebuke, but she didn't disagree. "Don't pick a fight with her today."

"If she'll be here tomorrow, I'll risk going home to my husband. No doubt *he's* eager for my company." Jessica handed the boy to Rebecca with a parting kiss. "Will you be here tomorrow when I come to call, Fanny?"

"I will be," she promised, still astonished by Jessica's outburst.

Jessica kissed Fanny's cheek perfunctorily before flouncing out the door.

Fanny stared after her. "What has gotten into her?"

"Marriage," Rebecca murmured. "She's not our quiet little mouse anymore."

"So I see."

"Also, she misses you. She misses all of us when we're away. Don't you remember how strange it was to leave home and suddenly be separated from the familiar? I think it might be worse for her, since her new home is so close by. We call upon Father first and must make the effort to call on her second. Milo took three days to make the stroll over, and Samuel still hasn't gone."

Fanny sighed heavily. "Marriage always

separates siblings, especially sisters. Surely she understands there's been no intentional slight meant toward her."

"She always had Father's ear and knew everything before we did for many years. She's lost that special place."

Fanny brushed her fingertip over her lips, thinking of the past. "I recall I was terribly lonely when I married and moved away."

"I was too," Rebecca agreed. "I had to make new friends."

Fanny moved to sit beside Rebecca. "Are you lonely again, now that you've married Rafferty?"

"No, I'm older, and Adam and I have many acquaintances in common. I have Ava to distract me, as well. Jessica will settle down when she has a child of her own to fuss over."

"You'll both have babes soon," Fanny noted, feeling oddly left out. "At least the distance between you is not so great that she'll have no one to turn to for advice when her time comes."

"Perhaps it will be me turning to her for help. I've never been pregnant before."

Fanny grinned. "*You*, taking advice?"

"On the subject of children, I always will." Rebecca tickled the boy under the chin. "I'm nervous, you know."

"About the child?"

"I worry that when I'm fat and cranky, the things Adam accepts about me will no longer appeal."

"I told you he's not the sort to abandon you."

"No, but I never thought that of Warner either and look what he did."

Fanny put her hand on Rebecca's shoulder and squeezed. "You'll make a wonderful mother, and already are the perfect wife."

"So would you—if you wanted to be."

Fanny signed. "That again?"

Rebecca settled the boy on her lap and the pair of them faced her as Rebecca spoke again. "I worry about you being alone. We all do."

"I'm not alone. I have a busy life, friends and my interests."

"Yes, you have been keeping very busy. But in a few years…?" Rebecca sighed. "Father will not live forever. Jessica and I might die in childbirth, or from ill health. Samuel could finally leave England as I've always suspected he would one day. And Milo, well, neither one of us has ever been close to him. Who will you have to comfort you in your old age? Who will you leave your wealth to?"

"To you, and Samuel and Jessica and Milo and—"

"I don't want your money." Rebecca's stare was piercing. "I want you to be happy."

"I promise you that I am. I'm doing exactly as I please and lack nothing," Fanny insisted.

"No, you're not truly happy. I think you were when Rivers was alive and never since."

Fanny had been completely and utterly devoted to her late husband. She hadn't cared about the number of years between their ages, as many other people had been. Rivers had been an exciting man, funny and wise. She'd had a complete life with him. He'd challenged her mind and her soul. "I miss him."

"Rivers is gone and you've chosen to carry on alone. But you can't live on remembered passions forever. Give love one more chance, I beg of you."

"I never gave up." Fanny smiled tightly. "But I think love gave up on me."

"Nonsense," Rebecca promised. "You will never find a man like Rivers again, so stop looking for him in the faces of those you meet."

"I'm not."

"Aren't you?" Rebecca handed Fanny the baby decisively.

Liam was a good weight for a child of his age. Fanny actually knew a lot about the raising of children since, as the eldest, she'd had a lot to do with her younger siblings' upbringing. She tucked Liam against her, assailed by the familiarity of the task…and a yearning she'd thought long buried.

"What is the first thing you consider when you make the acquaintance of a man?"

"Ah…" Fanny began, but Rebecca was on a roll and charged on.

"I'm sure you assess the quality of their clothes as a means to determine their wealth and status," Rebecca said, ticking off each point on her fingers.

Fanny rocked Liam from side to side. "Is that not a perfect way to uncover a fortune hunter?"

"There are good men who lack funds. Scoundrels can fall in love, too."

"Like Rafferty did with you," Fanny teased.

"You know how I felt about him once." Rebecca shrugged. "A more annoying man I have never met."

"And yet you have bound your life to his," Fanny noted. "You became his wife, never to be your own woman again."

"Marriage changes us all. Even you altered in so many ways," Rebecca noted.

"I did not."

"Oh, your habit of bringing home strays waned for a little while, but the impulse resumed once you didn't have Rivers to disapprove. During your marriage, you let longstanding friendships fall by the wayside. Was that a choice you made consciously, or did it just happen because his interests lied elsewhere."

Fanny gaped. "Are you done criticizing me yet?"

"It is a criticism I have laid at my own door. I changed because of Warner. I became critical of everything and everyone because of how he treated me. His actions brought to light every insecurity I possessed. I'm surprised anyone could stand me."

"You weren't so bad."

"I was a mean-spirited bitch," Rebecca confessed.

Fanny opened her mouth in shock to hear her sister use that word. "Becca! Language."

Rebecca giggled at Fanny's shock. "You can blame my new husband for my use of that word. He's made me an honest woman in every sense of the word. I highly recommend a second marriage to a scoundrel. They are very good for helping a lady loosen more than her corset."

"If you say so," Fanny replied, but she'd yet to meet a scoundrel she could like. The closest she'd come was an appreciation for an actor with a murky past and lock-picking skills.

"I do. Well, that is enough sisterly advice delivered for one day. I suppose I should return this young man to the nursery before the duchess scolds me for keeping him from his sleep. Unless you want to keep him."

"No, it would be wise to return him before you incur the duchess' wrath," Fanny murmured, laughing because Gillian was a gentle soul.

"I'll visit the duchess' chamber after that and see if I'm needed," Rebecca said. "Come find me before I go if you need to talk."

"I will," Fanny whispered as she caught sight of Jeremy Dawes striding past their door.

But that couldn't be.

Jeremy had left the estate yesterday. His room was empty, his fine clothes gone, too.

Fanny handed Liam to Rebecca quickly, keen to confirm that she hadn't just imagined seeing him.

Jeremy's parting remarks played through her mind again, as they had for all of last night. He'd suggested she was spoiled, acting as if she was entitled to take whatever and whoever she wanted without any care for their opinion. And he'd been right to a degree. There were few things she'd ever really cared about since becoming a widow.

But she cared about Jeremy Dawes.

All morning she'd tried to convince herself that she was better off without him, with no real conviction.

She stood, followed Rebecca to the base of the stairs, hoping to see him again. But her stomach churned with uncertainty at the knowledge he might have stayed. But what was he doing if he wasn't with her? And where had he spent last night?

She walked to the doorway of the library and looked around; but it was an empty room and there was no sign of him on any chair.

Disappointment crushed her.

But then Jeremy slid down a library ladder right next to the door she'd just walk through and she jumped ten feet in the air.

Despite the surprise, elation filled her. She *had* missed him. His easy company, his amusing banter. His presence in the room. His hands. She had worried that he'd traveled safely back to London on the stage. "Jeremy!"

"If you're looking for the duke, he'll be back in a moment." His tone was polite, but then his gaze slipped away.

Why hadn't Jeremy gone?

"That's fine," Fanny murmured, moving closer. "I was hoping we might talk."

Jeremy did not look pleased as he folded his arms over his chest and glowered. "What about?"

"Ah, Fanny. Just the woman I was hoping to talk to," Father said as he emerged from his study carrying a book. "Here, Dawes, this is what I was talking about earlier. Take a look through this and then go and show Samuel. He'll explain everything."

"Thank you," Jeremy said and then nodded to Fanny. "If you will excuse me."

And then he was gone.

Father strolled up to her side and put his arm about her shoulders. "I haven't seen you all day. Where have you been hiding yourself?"

"I was with Rebecca and Jessica just now. Jessica has gone home and Rebecca went above to see Gillian."

"Ah, I'm sorry to have missed them, but no matter." Father drew her toward his study. He shut the door, which usually meant he wanted no one to hear them talking or interrupt. She looked over her shoulder.

"Was there something you needed, Fanny?"

"Um, Father, what was Mr. Dawes doing in your library?"

"A bit of work for me. Nothing that concerns you." But everything Jeremy did concerned her. He was *her* friend not father's employee.

She gulped. "Mr. Dawes gave me the impression that he'd taken his leave."

"Is it so surprising that he hasn't?"

She stiffened. "We had a difference of opinion."

Father merely smiled. "That can happen."

She narrowed her eyes. "In truth, I thought he'd left me. I mean, that he'd left the estate yesterday."

"What? On foot?" As she nodded, Father started to smile. "He did leave…well, he tried to, but I encouraged him to stay a few weeks more."

"Weeks? Why would you do that?"

Father sighed. "Because there is love between you."

"What?!"

"Don't act so surprised. I've told you girls for years that you're all entirely loveable."

Fanny sank into a chair. "It's an absurd suggestion."

"Is it really?"

Father caught her hand, but she pulled away. "We hardly know each other."

"That never stopped you before." Father sighed. "I didn't realize you didn't believe in love at first sight anymore."

"It's preposterous. And you…you disapproved of our arrangement."

"I told you the truth. What you wanted to hear, only you didn't really listen. You always knew you had to end the affair and you went and did just that." Father sat down beside her. "It wasn't what I intended that Dawes would try to leave immediately."

She bristled at her father's attempt at manipulation. "I must have a separation of my private and public life."

"What makes you think there can be? Jeremy was never with you only because you had money, Fanny. You challenged him to want more for his life. He was happy with whatever crumbs you sent his way because he had a rare opportunity to experience another life for a while. And he thought he'd found a place supporting you. Becoming your friend. What else could he have done but leave when offered riches he's no right to nor desire for?"

"He…"

"Listen, love doesn't come along every day, my girl. That young man has more patience and practicality than anyone in society could ever have with you. You will always be rich, and you have become accustomed to getting your way. But not with him. No one can buy *his loyalty or love*."

Fanny lowered her face, ashamed that Father knew she'd tried.

Father put his arm about her again. "Yes, Jeremy has a past that we may never talk about or know completely. But as I understand it, he had no choice. He stole out of necessity until he found a better way to live. He changed for you. Improved himself to be worthy of standing in the same room as you."

Fanny gulped. "I don't know…"

But the words got stuck in her throat, and she couldn't finish. He *had* changed a lot. Agreed to everything she'd asked of him.

She had offered him money, compensation for sleeping with her, he'd said. It was a lot of money for someone like him to have turned down. Might he have made love to her without strings attached forever?

"There's only one way to find out if you could have a good life together," Father whispered.

"What do we even have in common?"

"A love of the theater. An appreciation of the outdoors. Vivid imaginations. Jeremy suggested a theater could be constructed in the woods for my next house party. I find I'm quite keen on the idea of putting on a play one year."

Fanny hadn't intended her arrangement with Jeremy to end badly, and it had gone in a direction she had feared. But it *was* over. Jeremy had said they were done in no uncertain terms, and she believed him. He had barely been able to look at her just now.

But as for the other of Father's suggestions, Fanny had never been looking for someone to love. Not Jeremy. Not a second time. Not after the pain of losing Rivers long before she was ready to be alone.

Jeremy was a young man in his prime, with no future but the one she'd thrust him toward. He had come to her bed, a somewhat reluctant lover in the beginning. He had expected her to grow bored with their arrangement at any moment, he'd said.

Except, she hadn't. And yet the moment their relationship had changed, and he'd interfered in her business dealings in fear for her safety around Wilks, she'd pushed Jeremy away.

But she shouldn't have. He was more cautious than she was about a great many things. She also enjoyed hearing Jeremy's views on the world, which were quite different from her experiences. His constant companionship made her feel content —safe—rather than smothered.

She wanted good things for him, and to be by his side to see his future unfold. Not separated by rules and society's conventions that would have disapproved of the relationship they'd shared.

They could not go back to the way things had been before they'd made love.

But could they go forward…together, if he was willing to trust her again.

In any adventure or investment opportunity, there was no way to know for certain how things would turn out. She'd been living from moment to moment for years. Doing exactly as she pleased. But those moments with Jeremy were some of the best of her recent years. She wanted more with him.

Father nudged her. "Fanny?"

"Yes, Father."

"He's a good man. He won't spend your fortune unwisely. I'd be surprised if he spent any, actually. And I'm prepared to sing his praises to society if need be, if he makes you happy," Father whispered.

Fanny bit her lip, considering her father's words. If Father was not difficult about Jeremy, her siblings might not be, either. Society would certainly talk for a good long while about such an unequal match. But then the novelty would wear off. No one would care in five or ten years what Jeremy's life might have been before they met.

But Fanny now had the chore of figuring out the state of her heart. No matter what Father said in favor of any match, Fanny would not be rushed to the altar a second time, or into any courtship either.

And even before any future of that sort could happen, Jeremy would have to forgive her and she'd have to convince him somehow that money was not all that mattered to her. He needed to know that he mattered more.

Chapter Sixteen

"Have you heard the news that Laughton repaired his fortunes on the 'change? He'll probably have his pick of next year's beauties on the marriage mart," Samuel said, riding along beside Jeremy with a loose-limbed confidence Jeremy utterly lacked.

Jeremy had no time to question how anyone made money on the *bloody 'change.* He was too busy clinging to the horse rolling about alarmingly under him.

"I wish him good hunting," Milo murmured sounding utterly bored of the topic already. Milo was on Jeremy's other side, riding one-handed with apparent disinterest for his horse's prancing antics or their destination.

Jeremy was utterly terrified and trying not to show his fear. Both men knew he'd no experience on a horse but had convinced him to come out with them anyway.

"Keep your heels down," Milo reminded him.

"And don't hold the reins so tightly," Samuel added. "You're on the estate's oldest plodding horse, and she'll go where we direct our horses and nowhere else."

"You say that, but I saw her roll her eyes," Jeremy warned. "That's bad, isn't it?"

Milo clapped Jeremy's horse on the rump. To his relief, the old mare didn't even flinch. "Molly is the perfect horse to learn upon. She'll look after you."

"I don't know why I need to start everything at once."

"You're on the horse because Father's note said you needed to be away from the manor for a while and you should start lessons with us."

Jeremy grumbled under his breath. "Stapleton's great plan to turn me into a gentleman is doomed to fail if I break my neck first."

"You're doing well," Samuel promised. "Just try not to think about falling off so much."

Milo chuckled. "Not far now."

Jeremy looked ahead and his mood brightened considerably to see the stables in sight again. "Thank God."

"Brother, I'd like to wish you good hunting, too," Samuel announced, returning to their earlier topic of conversation. "If you had any interest in making a match, I'd be there to support you. You do know it's time to marry again, don't you?"

"Was there a date set that I didn't know about," Milo asked, unsmiling. "It took Father years to replace mother."

"But he had all of us children to distract him when she died, so the succession was never in any serious doubt."

Milo shook his head. "I have no reason to remarry yet. The first marriage was quite enough trouble, thank you very much."

"But you need an heir," his brother shot back. "We all want to know the Stapleton estate and tenants will be looked after properly."

"You could always inherit."

Samuel seemed to choke. "I would love to oblige you but what a mess my boys would make of Stapleton if left to roam these pristine grounds forever."

"They'll grow out of their wild ways by the time they come of age," Milo promised, half smiling. "We did."

"Speak for yourself."

"Brother, you are too old for pretending your wild days are not far behind you."

"They don't have to be," Samuel replied mulishly. "All I'm saying is that you could go to London next season and take a look around. Run your eye over the ladies and see if anyone takes your fancy. If not, leave again and go back another year. It would please Father immensely to know you're thinking about the future. There's no need to be alone all your days just because your first marriage wasn't ideal."

"Ideal? No, it certainly was not even close to that. That is why I have no son." A bitter laugh escaped Milo. Clearly his marriage hadn't been good at all. But then a ghost of a smile flashed over his features. "I'm content with my life as it is, brother."

Jeremy, curious to know what made him smile so, spotted a maid wandering through the gardens.

"What do you say, Mr. Dawes? Are you in favor of marriage or remaining a bachelor forever? There's nothing wrong with keeping a regular woman in our beds, outside of marriage, eh?"

"I hadn't given it much thought," he replied. Well, he hadn't thought of marriage until yesterday's surprising conversation with the Duke of Stapleton. He didn't think marriage was in his future but kept that to himself. "What exactly is a regular woman? How do you find them?"

Milo laughed at his question. "A regular woman is one who doesn't ask when you will marry them."

"Don't listen to him, Dawes. All women wait for a marriage proposal," Samuel warned. "Some might even spring them on us poor bastards when you least expect it."

"I know what women want," Milo declared.

Jeremy shook his head quickly. "Not me. I find myself constantly surprised."

The pair laughed and clapped Jeremy on the back. Caught off guard, Jeremy nearly flew over the neck of his horse to be trampled. Jeremy quickly righted himself and tightened his legs around the horse's middle as he'd been warned to do.

"Poor fellow. You'll learn soon enough that

that's how they like to keep us all the time," Milo warned. "Companionship can always be found if you know where to look for it, though. We can even buy it for ourselves, if we must. Marriage is not needed to ensure satisfaction."

Jeremy looked at the pair curiously. "Is that how everyone in your family views matrimony? Like something to avoid rather than embrace?"

"It is a requirement for women if they wish to be considered respectable and for gentlemen who wish for legitimate heirs," Milo explained. "But most of my friends view it as something to avoid for as long as possible. I certainly should have."

They were approaching the stable block now and Samuel drew his mount closer. "Pull back on the reins slowly, that's it, and relax. The groom will hold Molly's head, so she won't wander off while you dismount. Now, wriggle your right foot free of the stirrup, throw your leg backward and dismount over the left side of your mount."

Jeremy executed what he thought was an adequate dismount, struggling because his left foot was still stuck in the stirrup, forgotten. Milo and Samuel did it with much more grace and speed. Jeremy gave the reins over to the groom with all possible haste and the horses were led away, much to his relief.

"Not bad for a first ride. Not bad at all. Just like a marriage really." Samuel grinned. "Exciting at first and not without highs and lows."

"Lots of lows," Milo grunted. "Marriage is not

for everyone. I was in love. But I was alone in that," he warned quietly.

Samuel sighed. "Perhaps the next woman you court won't pretend to be what she is not."

"I'd never marry a woman who claims to love me, now." Milo shook his head and then suddenly remembered Jeremy was listening. "Keep that to yourself."

Who could he tell that would care? "Of course."

He walked around the stable yard a bit, stretched his legs that seemed to have turned to jelly. He was supposed to find something to do with himself now until dinner that evening, he'd been told.

Fanny and the duchess were playing croquet on the lawn. It looked like great fun and he assumed she might be good at it, given the way she concentrated on every shot. He couldn't loiter, but he wished he could have a game.

"Are we boring you, Dawes?" Samuel asked quietly, coming up to stand beside him.

"Not at all."

The lord noticed the game underway. "We all used to play together when we were younger. Fanny would always win, having the cooler head, Rebecca would pout, and Jessica would sit herself down in the middle of play to stop the games from continuing if she wasn't winning, which was all the time."

"And if we were around," Milo said, coming up

to Jeremy's other side, "I'd beat Fanny, Samuel would annoy Becca so she missed, and Anna and Jessica would sit down to make us play around them."

Jeremy looked at Samuel and then at Milo. "Anna?"

The earl turned away and it was Samuel who answered. "Anna, our sister, was lost in childhood," he whispered.

"I'm sorry to hear that. My condolences."

The earl suddenly excused himself, leaving Jeremy and Samuel behind. "I didn't mean to upset him."

"He's never gotten over the loss. She was special. His favorite."

"Fanny has never mentioned she had another sister."

"It's a subject we never talk about very often, because then we lost mother too." Come let's find some shade and drink to forget life's disappointments."

"Mr. Dawes. Brother!"

Jeremy spun about at the sound of Fanny calling to them. She was rushing in their direction, skirts lifted over her ankles, hand holding down a hat on her head.

Samuel moved toward her. "Is something wrong?"

"Where are you going?"

"Dawes wanted a drink."

Fanny came to a stop. "I doubt drinking was

his suggestion, but it would be yours. I want to have a word with him. Do you mind excusing yourself?"

A sly smile crossed Samuel's lips as he looked between them. "Give him back in one piece."

Fanny wet her lips and then met Jeremy's gaze. "Might we stroll the garden together, sir?"

Jeremy shrugged, as if her request didn't bother him at all. But it did a little. "If you want."

They strolled off together, Fanny walking very slowly at his side. When they made a series of turns through the dense trees, at Fanny's behest, Jeremy heard her sigh. "What's the matter?"

"Nothing."

"It's never nothing when you sigh like that," he noted.

She frowned. "I do not sigh in any particular way."

He laughed softly at her indignation. "Yes, you do. There's one sort of sigh when you see a friend, another when you've a letter from your father," he leaned closer still, "and quite another when I put my lips to the back of your neck and kiss your skin."

Jeremy wrenched himself away from her and buttoned his lips, annoyed he'd fallen back into old habits so easily. Flirting with her had become second nature...but that was before she'd offered to pay him for making love to her.

"I've ruined our friendship, haven't I? I truly didn't mean to insult you."

"I didn't know what I'd signed," he admitted.

"But you did read it."

"No, I listened to you read it *to* me," he corrected. "I got lost in the sound of your voice and stopped paying attention long before you must have reached the end."

"I'll make sure you read every word in the future."

"The future?"

"*If* there's to be one," she said, then worried her lip. "Can you forgive me?"

"It probably *was* a mistake to hire me in the first place."

"No, it wasn't." She drew close. "We had a miscommunication, but the air is cleared now, isn't it?"

"You were bound to grow tired of my acting sooner or later," he admitted. "You should hire someone else for your next play."

"There isn't a good enough reason to pretend anymore," Fanny murmured. "No more acting for me."

They continued to walk and found themselves beside a field where a dozen workers toiled. Fanny waved at them and they waved back.

Jeremy smiled. "That's what I remember most about you on the day we met at the theater. You were kind to everyone, no matter their position."

"I remember you flirting with me until my sides ached from the laughter you inspired."

"Well, you were the prettiest lass in the room,"

he admitted. "I wanted to impress you, even before I knew who you really were."

"I was impressed. I still am." She looked down at her hands. "I see you've made friends with my brothers."

He smiled. "Does it look that way? I thought them more like conspirators to your father's torture."

"What torture?"

"Shooting at dawn. Riding. Living as a gentleman is hard work indeed when you have to worry about what everyone thinks and might say. How does anyone bear the scrutiny?"

"I don't always." When she turned, there was an uncertainty in her gaze he'd not seen before. "Most of the time I just don't care what anyone thinks."

"That is obvious."

"And I believed I'd made a mistake when I let you so close, you came to understand me so well. You played the part of an ardent suitor exceptionally well, Mr. Dawes. Better than I ever dreamed you might. But I do care what you think of me."

He glanced her way, saw that she was watching him closely. Waiting for him to render a verdict on her character. "You've a talent for acting yourself. Have you ever considered treading the boards?"

"No."

"That's a pity," he said with a quick smile.

"Shall we retrace our steps, my lady? Your family will be wondering where you are."

She moved to stand before him and clasped her hands together at her waist. "You've been spending a lot of time with my family, particularly my father."

Jeremy shrugged. "I like him."

She drew in a breath. "What I said to you yesterday, I truly apologize. I never should have offered you the money that way, even if I had promised it in the agreement. You do mean more to me than that. I mean…you mean something *else*, and it has nothing to do with money at all. Say again that you forgive me?"

He glanced her way again. Make her squirm, the duke had said. Yes, but for how long was such a measure necessary? His temper had already cooled. He'd overreacted by storming off with the intention of leaving the estate. He could have dealt with her and refused a penny with less fuss than he had stirred up. "What does it matter?"

"It matters very much to me."

He nodded. "Forgiven."

She inched closer a half step. "Can it ever be forgotten?"

Now that he wasn't sure of. His pride had taken a blow, and the *entire* family must know by now that she'd been willing to pay him for sex. The sum had been sufficiently large enough for him to only now feel a sense of unease that she could throw such an amount about so easily. Would she try to buy his affections and forgiveness in the future, too? It was an unpleasant possibility that she might try to end every disagreement they had that way. He wasn't so special to deserve any riches. "I don't know."

She gulped. "Father tells me he has invited you to stay."

Jeremy inclined his head. Since he had nowhere else to go at the moment, he saw no harm in staying for a while. He had started his lessons that morning with the duke's valet, who seemed to be possessed of a remarkable level of patience for Jeremy's limited abilities. He'd like to continue those lessons in secret, if only to help him not sign any more scandalous agreements.

Plus, the duke had suggested that Fanny had developed real feeling for him. An attachment she was afraid to admit to. He could understand her fears. He had them, too.

"For how long?"

"I don't rightly know. There is nothing pressing that draws me back to London for the moment."

Fanny started to walk, and after a moment he decided he would follow.

"You *should* stay. Take advantage of the country air and the friendships you've made here. You never know when a casual acquaintance might lead to an opportunity too good to pass up."

Fanny was attempting to manage him. Trying to alter the course of his life still. "Those friendships happen to be with your brothers."

"And Whitfield," she reminded him.

"Whitfield is your brother, too."

"Oh yes. Sorry. It's still odd to think of him that way. An adjustment. Everything is an adjustment. I'm not as adaptable to changes in my personal life as I am in business affairs."

There had been a level of intimacy, of sharing, between them that Jeremy had never experienced before he'd met Fanny. It was something he'd have to adjust to as well, if he stayed and continued to socialize with her and her family.

Suddenly, Fanny curled her arm through his. "When I found your room empty, I feared you had really gone."

Jeremy extracted himself from her grip. He wouldn't allow himself to slip back into too much familiarity with Fanny without this time knowing exactly what was in store for him. "What is it you want?"

"You." She wet her lips, clasped her hands at her waist and slowly looked up into his eyes. "I want a second chance with you…but I am afraid."

"Of what?"

"The day that I lose you."

Chapter Seventeen

Jeremy reeled back a step from her and Fanny's heart nearly pounded through her chest in fear that he'd laugh. Yes, she'd done it. Laid herself bare and damn the consequences of what many might see as a reckless admission on her part. She'd confided her worst fear to the man she admired above all others.

She had searched her soul after her talk with her father and decided he might know her better than she did herself. Father had made her see that her choice of casual flings had been an attempt to avoid being hurt by any loss ever again.

But Fanny could only be hurt if she lost someone she truly cared about. She couldn't bear to lose Jeremy. It would hurt so very much.

Jeremy, however, was frowning. "Why would you think you would lose me?"

Accident, misadventure, recklessness. "It's complicated."

"Isn't everything and everyone." He drew close. "I'm an orphan who has no idea where he came from. A youth who took advantage of anyone too lazy to guard their pockets." He gulped. "A fully grown man in his prime who can't even read, let alone understand the contract he signed with you."

Her eyes widened in shock. "What?"

"I've spent my life pretending to be someone I'm not," he said as he looked around them. "I am still pretending even today. I was a thief, Fanny. Now I'm playing the role of a gentleman, at home in such a glorious place. But I don't belong here."

"Yes, you do." She wet her lips again. "You belong with me. You stole my heart, Jeremy, a feat I believed impossible for so many years. I don't want to lose you. There is a way forward."

He sighed. "You never give up, do you."

"Not when I'm right," she vowed. She had been right about Jeremy in the beginning but had lost his trust when he'd expressed a different view of their relationship. Her money would never go away, and she felt it best to deal with that immediately. "I have money enough to last for the rest of our lives."

"I don't want charity, Fanny," he told her as he took hold of her trembling hands. "You should be with someone who will worship the ground you walk on, not your money."

"Then be with me. Not because you have no choice but because you do," she whispered.

"I have nothing to give you but a fortune in stolen moments like this."

"Those are enough," she promised. "Share them with me. Please."

"I've told you before that begging is beneath you." He scowled. "I never cared about your money, Fanny. I need to deserve a place at your side. I'd do anything you want to make you happy. Take on any role, as long as you do not try to pay me a fortune to do so."

"I can promise that."

"I had harbored a small hope that we might reconcile, and I have given the future some consideration as you've always urged me to do. Your father tried to put grand ideas in my head but I will make this very easy for you." He pulled a much-folded sheet of paper from his inner coat pocket. "I have taken the liberty of writing down what I feel I might need as an allowance each year to keep pace with you. Only for clothing and such. I want never to be an embarrassment to you or your family. If you feel I've made a mistake, please do correct my mathematics. I am not very good at finance, as you will find out soon enough."

Fanny didn't want to read the paper. She dreaded what she might find there. A husband could spend a fortune in one night of gambling.

But Jeremy seemed quite insistent, pushing the paper at her hand until she had to take it and read it.

The handwriting was inelegant, and every line sloped off toward the bottom of the page. She could read it, but only just.

A servant. Modest clothing allowance each year. A few pounds' pin money each quarter.

And that was all he asked for.

Fanny read the paper again, nearly disbelieving, and tears filled her eyes that Jeremy believed such a frugal sum could ever be considered excessive. It was too good to be true, but as she looked at him, she knew he meant never to be a burden.

In truth, he could have asked for ten times more than he had, and she'd willingly pay it, just to have the honor of being his. "Where would you like to live?"

Fanny had a large townhouse in London, the Rivers country estate near Bath, and another property overlooking the sea in Brighton that she hardly ever visited. Letterford and his bride would holiday there this year, but the next could be for them. They could go sea bathing and enjoy the solitude. But they would have to spend the season in London. The rest of the year could be lived anywhere, as long as they could be together.

"That is something I could not fathom. Of course, I want to be near you, but finding a room for a bachelor in Mayfair is an undertaking you might have to help me with. I don't know how close is close enough to suit you, or how great the cost might be."

The cost would be nothing to her, but she didn't want to pay for someone else to house him.

Jeremy living in her house would suit her best.

In her bed, always.

Forever.

Fanny smiled up at Jeremy. He hadn't even voiced the option of marriage, which was the only way they could be together every day. And it was, of course, the best situation if they were in love with each other, as Father claimed they were. "If you were close to hand, my heart would be easier."

He frowned. "I shall make enquiries the moment I return to London, but I am afraid the cost of my upkeep might be more than I budgeted for."

She took his hand in hers. Loving hands. The hands of a friend and a good man. "When *we* return to London, there will not be a need for you to seek out accommodations."

His eyes lit up. "You have a place in mind for me?"

"I do. My home."

The relief in his eyes diminished immediately. "That wouldn't be wise. You must think of your reputation."

"My reputation will remain beyond reproach if you were to ask for my hand in marriage."

He drew back. "I couldn't do that."

"I would say yes," she said, feeling certain of him now. They were negotiating for their future. A bargain she would honor for the rest of her life. She would adjust to being married again and heeding his warnings. He'd always listened to hers.

His once happy face became the quite the opposite, though. "No. Absolutely not."

"Why not?"

"Are you mad?" he demanded. "Why would you want to marry me?"

Fanny laughed softly. "There are so many reasons. But I do."

"You don't know me."

"I spent three weeks being courted before my late husband proposed. That's considerably shorter than the length of our acquaintance. What I need to know about you, you will tell me one day soon, I trust."

He frowned again. "Will I now?"

"People who love each other tell each other everything." Fanny nodded. "Oh, yes. This is most certainly a love worth fighting for, sir. I know you feel it, too."

He was silent for several minutes, considering, imagining she hoped, a different sort of role for himself in her life.

Fanny was handing him the world, her world, and her vast fortune on a platter if they wed, and she respected him all the more for having serious misgivings about taking her on. They would love each other, and they would fight, too. He'd question her and she'd push him to reach for his dreams.

When he was silent too long, she drew closer to him. "Are you really going to claim that you don't want to spend the rest of your life flirting with me?"

"We don't have to marry for that," he offered. "We could keep seeing each other. We'd find a way to meet discreetly somewhere every few weeks."

"I would rather not sneak around any longer."

While she was disappointed that Jeremy didn't jump at the chance to marry her, she was glad he wasn't rushing to accept her suggestion either without proper consideration. But surely he knew her well enough to understand she did nothing halfway. "I'm not asking you to give up your career, and I know, too, I am not the woman you might have imagined marrying, but I assure you, I am constant. My feelings for you will only grow the longer we are together."

"How would you feel about a long courtship, then?"

She studied him. She enjoyed a good negotiation. "For how long?"

"As long as we've known each other," he suggested. "Six months."

"No, that is much too long. I only had to wait a month before I married River," she explained.

"It's long enough for you to really consider whether you want to marry a pauper. And besides, your family is in mourning."

"Two months," she countered, warming to the challenge of convincing him to marry her more quickly.

"Four. That's long enough for me to learn to ride a horse and not be in danger of falling off. I've heard it's a requirement of being a gentleman about Town to ride every morning. I'd rather not break my neck in Hyde Park. In three months, your family will be out of mourning and the banns can be called."

"So, we agree to marry in three months."

"No. I said four." He shook his head, halting her attempt to bring the date forward with a clear decision on his part. "If we *were* to marry, I should like to have Mrs. Hawthorne attend our wedding celebrations. We will delay to give the widow time to grieve before we ask her to be happy for us. She wanted so much to attend your wedding."

"That is very considerate of you." She should have thought of that herself. "I just want us to be together. You'll stay with me in Mayfair when I return to Town."

"Not a chance." Jeremy looked down upon her, his expression serious. "I'll stay where the duke suggests I should stay and visit you every day. I am, as ever, at your complete disposal."

Fanny wasn't sure if Jeremy's reliance on Father's opinion was in her best interests or not but if she could see Jeremy every day, Fanny could still do her work and have time to enjoy introducing him to her friends. Jeremy was worth the effort of making an agreement that he was comfortable with. "Agreed, and when I need to travel, you will accompany me."

"Along with a suitable chaperone to protect you from any gossip," he added with a smile.

A chaperone would seriously impede any encounters of a romantic nature between them. But if Fanny chose a chaperone from among her most liberal-minded widowed friends, she was sure she and Jeremy could meet under the sheets as often as she wished during any house party they might attend together. The appearance of respectability was all that really mattered to society. When they married—and she couldn't imagine he'd change her mind now—she would have Jeremy all to herself. "Daily meetings, three months of courtship, and marriage by banns on," she did a quick calculation in her head adding in the period for the reading of the banns, "approximately the twenty-first of November. It's a deal," she said, putting her hand out.

"Let's not put that in writing this time." Jeremy sighed as they shook. He held her hand and brought her closer to him. When he leaned down, it was just like the first time, when he'd almost kissed her. "You love me," he whispered.

"Deeply." Her eyes dropped to his lips, where a smile lingered.

"It's about time." His eyes lifted to hers and then he smiled somewhat shyly. "I have loved you from the moment I met you. I tried so hard to master my role of a smitten suitor in a bid to impress you that I never was acting the part. But I never imagined you'd come to care for me as well."

Fanny pushed herself against his body and rejoiced when his arms encircled her waist finally. "You love me. Say it again."

His lips twitched as he lowered them inches from hers, "You love me."

She laughed softly. "Deeply and forever."

Jeremy cupped her face, tilting her lips up to

his so they hovered on the verge of a kiss. He caught her gaze, holding her stare a long moment. "People will talk."

"People always do. Some will declare that I've finally been tamed."

"My dear lady, taming you is the last thing on my mind."

And then like any great romantic hero of the stage, he tipped her backward over his arm and kissed her soundly. For a moment, Fanny could swear she heard the sound of distant applause.

Epilogue

Mayfair, London
14 February, 1820

Jeremy flicked through the stack of letters he'd been handed with a severe frown as he stood in the dim hall of Fanny's exquisite Mayfair home. He marched into the adjoining room. "Fenton, has my wife not seen the mail yet?"

Fenton didn't rise as usual, but the evil goose at his feet did. Jeremy had learned to keep clear of the pair.

"Not as yet, Mr. Dawes. She's still in her meeting with Mr. Danvers."

Even before their marriage, Fanny and Jeremy had got their heads together and decided the faithful Stapleton steward needed a change of scenery. Fenton's health had been causing concern. He was cross with everyone, until Fanny had tricked a confession out of him. *Gout.*

Fanny, a favorite, had stolen Fenton away from her father's employ for an easier occupation with them. His job was to sit about with his stick and glare at anyone who sought to impose themselves on Fanny when Jeremy was not around and take care of the evil goose roaming the house. "I did hear voices raised earlier, sir, but it's become quite again for the last half hour."

Jeremy looked at him sharply. "Did you interrupt like I asked you to?"

"Of course. I had a pair of our largest footmen carry the tea tray and dole out the cups very slowly. That seemed to calm things down. The door was left open after that, and they remain outside in full view of her visitor even now."

Jeremy glanced toward her study to see for himself. "Good."

Fanny had been in the meeting when he'd gone out to meet members of her family for a ride in Hyde Park hours ago. He hoped things were going her way at last. This particular transaction, the sale of Cedar Mill, had been keeping her awake at night in recent weeks. He didn't like it when she tossed and turned. It wasn't good for her health or his plans.

It had been weeks since she'd spent a whole day with him. He hoped she'd be finished soon because since it was Valentine's Day and he wanted to entice her to forget her worries with serious idleness and indulgence.

He retraced his steps to the hall and looked toward his wife's study where she conducted all business meetings—without him.

The footmen nodded that all was well now. Jeremy was doing his best to make it clear that his wife was not without protection at all times. If he could have stayed and been of any help to her, he would have canceled the plans he had made with her family. But he'd found supposedly intelligent men tried to defer to him instead of Fanny when it came to any business dealings.

So he absented himself from all important decision-making meetings, but he was interested in what Fanny was doing with the money, but he was hardly in charge of how it was spent and never would be. The fortune was still Fanny's money, in his opinion, even if she tried to convince him it was his, too. She retained full command of her fortune despite them being husband and wife.

He did not mind that other men whispered he was henpecked. Jeremy simply knew his limitations and worked around them. He wasn't smart enough to manage thousands of pounds and dozens of properties across the country. He remained in awe and proud of Fanny's achievements. "Would you subtly let my wife know that I have returned."

"I don't know that subtle will be enough, but I'll do my best. Danvers has a tongue hinged in the middle." Fenton complained. "I trust the duke is in good health."

"Fine form as usual. We're invited to a late luncheon with the duke and duchess tomorrow, so we'll need the carriage brought round at a quarter to two o'clock, and for Fanny's maid to be ready at short notice to change her into a suitable gown. I trust you didn't forget the surprise I planned begins tonight."

His first Valentine's Day with someone he loved deserved a special celebration. Jeremy hadn't had to think too hard to decide what to do. An evening of togetherness: dinner and wine in bed, and perhaps an early night for the love of his life. He'd issued orders that they were not to be disturbed once Fanny came up to their rooms unless someone was dying.

He wouldn't allow Fanny to think of anything but herself tonight.

The servant went off, and Jeremy climbed the staircase, admiring the opulence and Fanny's good taste. Of all her properties, this one held a special place in his heart. It was the first home he'd ever been in where he felt he belonged.

But after a ride in the park and a long talk in the duke's stables, he smelled of horses and other manly odors he'd rather be rid of. A servant had run ahead and filled his copper tub already, so he climbed into the steaming bath and scrubbed away at his skin and hair with plain soap, before drying himself with a length of soft cloth.

He was just putting on a robe when his wife hurried in, carrying a stack of papers against her chest. "I've done it. Cedar Mill is sold!"

Jeremy strolled to Fanny and dropped a kiss on her cheek, and then took the stack of papers from her. "Congratulations."

"I cannot believe it's finally done and I got my original asking price, too."

"Danvers was a fool to believe you were desperate to offload the mill just because of the little stir Thwaite stirred up over me."

"Yes, Thwaite tried his best to sour the deal and now must count the cost. I have it on good authority that several prominent matrons gave him hell over the vile gossip he was spreading. As if I would ever need to pay a man to share my bed," she said, grinning impishly at him.

"Ridiculous," he agreed. "I have to beat back your admirers every day."

"The only man I want is you."

Jeremy put her papers away in the large safe he'd had installed in her chambers and locked it before turning to face her. "Now, which do you want first? Bath, dinner or bed?"

"I am a bit tired," she admitted "But I want to hear about your day now. How was my father?"

"He made me laugh."

She smiled. "What did he say that was so funny?"

Jeremy glanced at his wife. The Duke of Stapleton had become more father than a friend to Jeremy, who'd never had either really. Stapleton was always doling out bits of sage advice, but his most frequent topic of late was discussing when Jeremy and Fanny would make a grandfather of him. The duke had today claimed Jeremy was tardy at keeping up his side of their bargain.

Jeremy had taken great pleasure in reminding him there was no written proof of any such bargain being made. A babe took time and would come when that time was right, and not a moment before anyway. "So many things. We're to have luncheon with them tomorrow," Jeremy warned. "I believed there was nothing in your calendar when I accepted."

"I have no plans for tomorrow besides sleeping late now that the mill is sold." She looped her arms around his neck. "Nothing but being with you like this. Happy Valentine's Day, my love."

Fanny drew his head down and kissed him quickly.

"I like the sound of that, and the way you taste. May I have another kiss, darling?"

"You can."

While they kissed, Jeremy slid his hand down her back until he reached her rear. He squeezed and kneaded her rump and then decided to put his hands all over her before his special dinner would arrive. There was just enough time to indulge her passions and do a proper job of it. She always smiled more after he made love to her.

He was working his way up her spine, unfastening her from her gown when she spoke. "Jeremy, how do you feel about cutting short the season and spending a few months at Stapleton this summer?"

He pressed a kiss to her neck. "I'm easy either way. You know that."

"Good. I think having my family around would be good for us."

He drew back and stared at her. "Why?"

She patted his chest. "I might be increasing."

Jeremy gaped, and then he whooped in joy, caught Fanny up in his arms and spun her around and around. "*Devil take it*! A babe? That'll make the duke happy."

"So, you don't mind?"

"Mind? Are you mad, woman? I can hardly wait."

She bit her lip. "I was afraid it was too soon. You're just finding your feet in society, and there's your new play, too. A baby will change how much time we spend in Town."

He swooped down to kiss her. "Nothing could make me happier than to spend a year in the country. I hope our daughter will be as smart and as beautiful as her mother."

"I hope our *son* will make me laugh like his father always can." But then she frowned. "What does my father's happiness have to do with our child?"

Jeremy laughed. "You're jesting. It's his favorite topic of conversation. Doesn't he pester you about it, too?"

"No. Actually, I was surprised to realize that Father hadn't brought up the possibility with me when we married," she said with a laugh.

Jeremy grinned, his heart full. "With all that is on your plate, I suppose he didn't want to add to your worries if it never happened. He told me his concerns last year before we decided to wed."

Fanny squinted at him. "Is his advice why you're always trying to keep me in bed in the mornings after we make love?"

Jeremy shrugged. "The duke *has* mentioned conception sometimes needs a little help, but that's not why I keep you in our bed."

Her eyes narrowed even more. "Why then?"

Jeremy grinned. "Pure selfishness. The minute your feet hit the floor, you'll put on clothes and pin up your hair, and I have to share you with everyone else."

He brushed his fingertips down her spine. He loved it when it was just the two of them, and naked, but Fanny needed more in her life than just a husband. Now he would have more, too.

She touched his face. "Jeremy dear, even when I'm not with you and working, I think of you."

"I believe you." Jeremy brought her hands up to his mouth and kissed her knuckles. "A baby to love. Can this be happening?"

Her eyes narrowed again. "A baby that my father will try to steal away to play with the minute we turn our backs," Fanny warned.

"I don't mind. At least our child will know he has a grandfather who cares about him."

Fanny sighed. "He, or she, will know their parents love them, too."

Jeremy finished undressing Fanny and drew

her to the bed. "You know, the duke has been telling me about your mother and how he took care of her when she was increasing. He said he spent every night rubbing her back and legs, in the last weeks before you were born."

"You really can't go wrong with Father's advice on the subject when it sounds like that."

He eased Fanny down until she was flat on her back and then climbed up on their bed with her. He put his hands on her stomach and lowered his head to kiss her belly.

But the babe was still too small to be noticeable, so he turned Fanny over and kneaded the tightness in her shoulders away, the way he often did after a long day at her desk.

Fanny sighed deeply and let out a grateful moan, too.

"You know, if I can do half as well as your father, I'll consider myself a good husband."

Fanny turned to look up at him. "You are a good husband now. I got lucky the day I met you."

"I'm the lucky one." He leaned down to Fanny's ear to whisper, "But you haven't seen me at my best yet. Just wait. You are going to be so spoiled in the years ahead. I promise to never stop loving you. No matter how round you get."

Fanny laughed softly. "I'll hold you to that when I'm only capable of waddling and get stuck in a chair the way Rebecca did at Christmas."

"I promise to love you no matter what," Jeremy

vowed. He went to work on Fanny's back, kneaded away the stresses of her day. When she was nearly asleep, he gently turned her and she smiled dreamily up at him. And Jeremy considered himself the luckiest man alive—he'd found somewhere to belong.

If you enjoyed this story don't miss the rest of
the Saints and Sinners series…

The Duke and I

The Duke of Stapleton abhors Christmas nonsense, but could a kiss exchanged under mistletoe with his daughter's shy companion alter his opinion of the season?

A Gentleman's Vow

To thwart an unwanted admirer, Lady Jessica Westfall enlists the aid of Gideon Whitfield, her dearest friend…and the love she's unknowingly sought all along.

An Earl of Her Own

Rebecca Warner has no time for the maddening Lord Rafferty. Until the earl proves her most ardent ally—both in and out of his bedchamber.

More Regency Romance...

Distinguished Rogues Series
Book 1: Chills
Book 2: Broken
Book 3: Charity
Book 4: An Accidental Affair
Book 5: Keepsake
Book 6: An Improper Proposal
Book 7: Reason to Wed
Book 8: The Trouble with Love
Book 9: Married by Moonlight
Book 10: Lord of Sin
Book 11: The Duke's Heart
Book 12: Romancing the Earl
Book 13: One Enchanted Christmas
Book 14: Desire by Design
Book 15: His Perfect Bride
Book 16: Pleasures of the Night

...and many more

About Heather Boyd

USA Today Bestselling Author Heather Boyd believes every character she creates deserves their own happily-ever-after—no matter how much trouble she puts them through. With that goal in mind, she writes steamy romances that skirt the boundaries of propriety to keep readers enthralled until the wee hours of the morning. Heather has published over 40 regency romance novels and shorter works full of daring seductions and distinguished rogues. She lives north of Sydney, Australia, with her trio of rogues and pair of four-legged overlords.

You can find details of her work at
www.Heather-Boyd.com